CW00470401

A Slice of Excitement

BRIAN BANHAM

A CIP catalogue record for this book is available from the British Library.

ISBN: 978-1978361010

CHAPTER 1

We arrived at the hotel. It had a long entrance hall leading up to reception, I checked in under my name and gave the receptionist my passport... After being assured we did have a suite, with a terrace looking out over the sea, we made our way to the lift, both silent. I was heavily loaded with my case and photographic equipment. She was carrying a very small, light case and handbag. The entrance room of our suite was large, well furnished, with double doors leading onto the terrace. The bedroom was dominated by a king-sized bed, a sliding door also led onto the terrace, where there were two easy cane chairs.

"Hope it keeps fine." I grunted, the evening sun was shining directly into our suite, still warm nearing the end of summer.

She had put down her case and after looking left and right on the terrace, settled into one of the chairs. "I would like to be alone for a few minutes," she said.

I needed to visit the bathroom and left her alone. I then hung up my suit, emptied my case, and generally placed my equipment and other clothes where I could easily get them. I went into the bathroom, sat on the chair beside the bath, and contemplated the situation. I was in Nice to cover the launch of a new car. I would be photographing the stills and the film crew, who were making a commercial using the car, would arrive on the red eye the next morning. I had insisted with the agency that I was not flying; my last two experiences had been so ghastly, that I was now determined not to fly anywhere in Europe that could be reached by road or rail.

I had met my companion in the dining car on the train, having slept overnight in Paris, arriving there on Eurostar. I was planning an early lunch but, so had many of the other travellers, and there was only one table left with two seats, one of them occupied by a strikingly attractive lady. She was wearing what appeared to be sunglasses, or maybe they just turned brown, but it wasn't that bright… I shuffled a bit, then plucked up courage and asked if she would mind if I joined her. She nodded and gave a glimpse of a smile as I slid into the small space. Almost immediately an immaculate waiter appeared with a menu, and asked if I wanted an aperitif. My French was passable but rusty. "A beer would be fine please. Can I offer you a drink?" I enquired of my companion.

"Non Merci, I am having a glass of wine with my lunch."

I wondered how she would react to introducing myself, I would try my simple French. "I guess that as we are to be together for a while, it might be helpful to introduce myself; my name is Alan, Alan Sears."

"Maria," then she looked down at the book she was reading. I had the Times from the previous day and made a pretence of doing the Sudoku, but my heart wasn't in it, and as a basket of bread arrived on the table with my very small beer, I settled into munching some of the bread, sipping my beer, and gazing out at the scenery flashing past. As I was about to select my lunch I asked if she had any recommendations. She looked up from her book, gave a sigh of resignation, and said, she didn't often travel by train, so was not able to help. I then gave my order and also included a bottle of Puligny Montrachet. As she had virtually finished her glass of white wine, I asked if she would like a glass of mine as it arrived.

She said, "thank you I like your choice, but it's pronounced using the T. Its Puligny Montrachet, but the T is soft." I smiled to myself.

"Thanks, I've been drinking this and others for years, but you have just exposed me." She also spoke immaculate English I noticed. We were able to talk over a delicious meal, where did UK trains stand in the reckoning? The usual trolley pushed through the trains, loaded with bread rolls, pies, and crisps, perhaps the odd dining car on long journeys. I made a point for French rail dining experience, which she agreed with. "Where are you going?" she enquired.

I told her I was going to Nice to cover an advertising session with a new model Renault. "I am a photographer, and we have a three day programme including commercials. The film unit is flying down tomorrow morning."

"Do you enjoy that sort of work, publicity, photos, advertising?"

"Well yes and no," I replied, "financially very rewarding, artistically challenging."

"Is that your main work?"

"No, but on an assignment like Nice for three days, I am contented."

"Do you travel much?" She asked.

"Yes, I also have a contract with a major Oil Company which has meant I've clung to a buoy in the gulf of Mexico, been on a wooden barge in China eating, (jam sandwiches), frozen in the sea off Norway, and also been to many other remote parts of the world."

"So are you settled with a family?"

"No I am a nomad," I added a smile, "in fact I've

travelled so much, that I don't get to spend a great deal of time in any country now it seems. And what about you, where are you headed?"

"I'm not really headed anywhere. I'm getting away."

"You must be headed somewhere, this train eventually stops in Nice."

"Well then that's where I'm headed."

I tried to work out what she was saying. "Do you live in Paris?"

I waited for a response.

"Yes I've been there several years now."

"Your English is so good, are you French?"

"Part," she said with a smile.

I was beginning to enjoy the game, "I do believe you are teasing me."

"Is that easy?" she asked.

I refilled my glass and offered more to her, she thanked me and said, "just a finger or two."

"That's an English thing, just a finger or two."

"Well you are bringing out the maiden in me!"

"OK, where did you school? I bet a posh English home counties."

"You're right on one count."

"Which, the English, or home counties?"

"The English. I was actually born and brought up in Whitby, and went to one of Yorkshire's best. It was so good I couldn't wait to go abroad, and France beckoned."

"What did you study? You're obviously an artist of some sort."

"What do you mean. Of some sort?"

"Well that's not a very flattering thing to say but, your dress, your appearance, your whole attitude says artistic."

"I studied design and drama."

"I knew it."

4

"When I first came to France, Paris, I did a variety of fashion jobs, a bit of modelling, but I'm too squat now to show off clothes. You've not seen me standing up yet, have you?"

"Can't wait," I said.

"Thanks, if I did stand up and walk away, what would you say?"

"I'd chase after you and say, hey you better pay your bill."

She smiled. "Yesterday I almost took a vow of silence, I felt so low I thought I would just disappear for a while and spend time totally alone. Thank you for rescuing me, but, I should go back to my seat and recover."

"What does that mean?"

"I feel I need to reflect on my present situation, and maybe a few days solitary will straighten me out."

"Do you want to tell me?"

"I've enjoyed our conversation, but I don't feel up to enlightening you on why I am travelling somewhere without having any particular place to go."

"You could spend the next three days with me if you feel like it, no strings, just friendship, and you might get some film food, bacon sarny's, or dogs, and plenty of coffee. Then if you want to confess during that time, I would be all ears."

"I don't think confess is the right word."

"No I know, that was just slapstick. I've enjoyed our talk. We've probably got another couple of hours before we get to Nice; I would be very happy to get another bottle of P with a soft T and just let's pass the time of day, without any need to think too deeply. I imagine that whatever has sent you off to be alone has something to do with a fella. It wouldn't be murder would it?" I said with my widest smile.

For a brief moment she looked tense, then her smile took over.

"My gun is strapped to my left hip buster, so watch out. I would have liked to have a shoulder holster, but that's for cowboys and spies."

"Is Paris relaxed? Every magazine that is in the arts says, Paris is very competitive, and you have to be very on the ball in clothes or art to make it there."

"Yes it is competitive, I think in all aspects of art particularly, but it still claims that most of the leading fashion designers are very happy to show in Paris, although London now has a good reputation."

"I've not covered much in the way of fashion, I think I'm more of a husky photographer, somehow can't see myself doing a David Bailey on some skinny six foot fifteen year old model."

"That's wishful thinking, models now earn enormous amounts, and they all have security guys on tap. Their whole existence is planned, what to eat, how to look, how to walk- it's tough."

"I'll get another bottle" I said, not wanting to get in too deep on modelling or fashion.

"Ok then, you've persuaded me."

We both relaxed and spent a little time looking at the scenery as we were travelling through some majestic countryside; a wonderful mountain view was rushing past.

The new bottle arrived I topped up our glasses and I toasted Maria.

"*I've just met a girl called Maria and suddenly that name will never be the same again.* Phew, wish I could sing."

"Thank you your voice is good?"

We talked through the next two hours and then we were pulling into Nice.

"I have a suite in one of the hotels overlooking the sea, all provided with the job. Will you join me, no strings, just friendship."

She pondered this and I started to worry that it was goodbye, but suddenly she produced a wide smile and said. "Yes but it will only be separate rooms."

"The suite has that I'm sure, and I'm hoping for a terrace to watch the big yachts going past." We were both a little bit tiddly as we walked off the platform. I smiled to myself, inside I was already excited. We caught a very expensive taxi to the West End Hotel, close to the splendid Le Negresco. Found our way to the sixth floor and our suite. Maria went out to the small terrace.

I telephoned reception and asked for a key to the mini bar as it was locked. "What do you want Monsieur?"

"Well perhaps a half bottle of champagne, some white wine, maybe a Chablis, a couple of beers and some cashew nuts, and can you ensure that these will be in the fridge each day? I am here for possibly three days."

"Yes Mr Sears, I know that and it will be OK."

I glanced out of the window, Maria appeared to be sleeping, well perhaps she's not used to drinking a bottle of wine plus at lunch time I thought, best to leave her and maybe I will have a doze myself. I was also intrigued and keen to get her to tell me why she was intent on 'getting away,' as she had said earlier. What was she getting away from? She looked as if she was comfortably off, but had not as yet spent anything, as I had paid for our lunches and wines.

I looked at my contract and timing for the photo shoot, then laid out on the bed, having removed my shoes. Within minutes I was asleep to be wakened I thought by a door being shut. I looked out to the terrace and no Maria, I quickly checked my jacket to see if my wallet was there, and it was, then I noticed a little note lying beside the bed, I picked it up and read. "Alan I have to do a bit of shopping, I will be back soon...don't fret, I am happy to be in your care for a few days."

At that moment the door buzzer went and I thought she's back, but it was a service girl. Tall elegant and absolutely beautiful, "I have your mini bar things, can I come in?"

I stood back, she pushed her trolley in and proceeded to replenish the fridge. When she finished she asked me if I was staying long.

"Yes for three, maybe more days."

"Do you know Nice?"

"Well I've been here a couple of times on a long weekend break, both times in the summer and have enjoyed the town and the sea, except you have pebbles, where you should have sand on the beach."

"You can always wear those rubber shoes that everyone has nowadays."

"Um," I said, and realised I was talking in English and she was perfect.

Was I getting a come on sign from her. She looked at the photographic equipment I had and asked the obvious. "What are you doing?"

I told her and then she suddenly excused herself and said, "I have other rooms to service. I hope you enjoy Nice."

I looked at myself in the mirror, in one day I had found myself being looked at a little longingly, by beautiful females, or was I kidding myself? and it was exciting. My image looked just as it had when I set off yesterday. Is this going to be an adventure?

I decided that a shower would be good, but what if Maria came back whilst I was singing…Then I noticed that the key to the door was not on the dressing table anyway, so I guess she must have taken it.

I went into the bathroom and stripped off, the shower head was huge and the water poured down on me with some force. I stood in it for some minutes letting it revive me from the alcohol excess, I was drying myself when I heard a call from the room. It was Maria. I draped the towel around me, combed my hair, had a quick glance in the mirror, and came out. Still wearing her sunglasses, she was holding a bunch of flowers and also had a small bag. "They're beautiful, your flowers." I said.

"You should see in the bag, I have something for you."

I sat on the bed and said. "Go on spoil me, what have I done to deserve this, whatever it is?"

She laughed and said, "close your eyes," I did, "now open them." Lying in her hand was a silk tie, it's background of deep blue with faint green flowers decorating it all the way up.

"That's great," I murmured, "that's very kind of you."

"No not kind, that's the way you would thank an old aunt. I wanted to give you something that you would remember me by, you have been so generous with your time and lunch and not questioning me as to why I am running away from something. I feel much better already, and I may be able to face up to the future, when yesterday I was convinced there was no future."

"That's pretty deep," I said.

"I would like a shower then could we visit the old town and maybe sit on the beach," she said.

"Sure, maybe find a club or dancing."

"No I would much prefer a quiet evening, just the two of us, maybe just relax."

"Fine by me, my call isn't until nine am tomorrow, so a relaxing evening, right up my street." We both kept off the fact that there was only one huge bed, but the settee in the sitting room looked as if it could be made up as a bed, but in the back of my mind I had other thoughts. How would she react to any suggestion of shared bed?

I did my usual sudoku as she showered. I heard a few

gasps as presumably she had the water too hot, but she eventually came out of the bathroom draped in a large towel and a plastic bath cap. "What do you think of the head gear?" she asked.

"It's added something wild and wonderful with a touch of amnesia." I replied.

"I like that," she said.

"What the wild, or amnesia?"

"I like them both, in all my years of flirting I have never been flattered like that."

"I must work at this."

"I'm getting dressed then we can take a walk," she said.

"OK."

After a few minutes she appeared in the same clothes but with a beautiful light scarf round her neck and the sunglasses. She really was beautiful, lovely eyes, brown hair long and slightly waved, tumbling over her shoulders, her figure was full in all the right places, and she had superb legs.

I took all this in at a glance, well maybe a lecherous stare.

I had spent several hours already with her and I was only just beginning to really appreciate her.

"Do you think it's going to be cold?" I asked keeping my voice level.

"No, but I was just showing off my wardrobe before we set out. Can we go to the old town? I've never been and I have read there is something for everyone there."

"It's some time since I've been, but it has a great atmosphere, I don't think I will need to eat much."

She agreed. I was feeling better from my sleep and shower, and looking forward to seeing a bit of Nice. The slanting sun was still shining on the balcony, she draped her scarf over one of the chairs, fiddled with her dark glasses, then we shut our door and ventured down in the lift. We stepped out from the hotel into the lovely warm atmosphere from the evening sun, as we did so I noticed a man on the pavement staring at us. I took Maria's arm and we wondered off.

"You did say earlier that we could hold hands." I muttered.

"Did I?" she said. "Maybe it was while we were drinking, and I felt that we could have a sort of tourist moment."

"Oh and I thought romance was in the air."

"Alan, let's just be friends on a stroll, if I happen to slip my little hand into your great paw, you mustn't grip it too tightly, OK?"

I took that as a moment of progress, I was certainly enjoying her company and presence, she was beautiful and the dark glasses added to her attraction. I was unattached, having just finished an extremely active and demanding time with an Australian model. She had just returned to her country without any future promises from both of us. Initially I missed her, she had been gone for two weeks, but work and a chance to recover my energies had been very welcome.

Nice old town kept us both interested as we wandered round the flower stalls, art galleries, and shops. All open and busy. Several people were sitting out at bars and cafes, and I ventured that perhaps we might enjoy a glass of champagne. We settled into two very comfortable wicker chairs and watched the crowds wandering by. Many years previously on holiday with friends, in France, two of us had gone to Bandol in the south, and my friend had initiated me into 'people watching' as a productive pastime. He was correct. This was becoming very enjoyable.

I started to tell her what I expected my photographic job would entail, That I had been booked for three days, but would certainly have time to spend with her in Nice if that suited her.

"Perhaps you can tell me more about yourself?" she suddenly asked.

"Well have you got a month, no maybe three weeks will do."

She smiled. "How about an hour."

"Better top up our champagne then."

"I was born in Norfolk, a little village with a church, two pubs, a shop, and a sewerage farm, care of the USA, built when the war was on. Actually it's set in what we Norfolkers call a forest, but it's really a plantation. We don't have many forests in Norfolk, well apart from the babes in the wood forest, which was quite close to where I was born. Wayland Wood is reputed to be it. So we tend to exaggerate everything when there is the odd tree. The sewage farm is about half a mile from the village so we weren't overcome with odours!! We were about twelve miles from Norwich, the city of culture and Canaries. Did you know Norwich in the 16th century was the second largest city in England?"

She smiled at that. "Never been to Norfolk, should I?"

"That's debatable. My dad is a farmer and my mother owns the village shop. I went to Thetford School and amongst other things concentrated on geography, so I can tell you without fear of contradiction about the match striking industry in Sweden."

"Do they smoke in Sweden?" she smiled.

"After school I got a job in Norwich working with a small advertising company, I was a bit like a fish out of water, but developed a real interest in photography and after some success, mainly through the good offices of the advertising company decided to go to London, 'where the streets are paved with gold.' Doing the same sort of work, and two years ago set up my own studios, albeit in need of paint and money but, I've been very lucky, and got involved with commercials through a friend and agent. Did a bit of modelling work and now you see me in all my glory."

"Wow that's a quick resume, you've still got most of the hour left."

"Ok there's been the odd furrow on me brow, and a bit of bread and pullet, that's another Norfolk expression. But things are ok and here I am in Nice, with just about the perfect evening ahead of me."

"That's a bit flattering."

"No I am very relaxed with you and I want a bit more of your background now."

"I'm not ready, I have told you that I have been in Paris for some time and yesterday (gosh was that yesterday). I decided to leave. Maybe I will tell you before we part."

"Will you stay on then?"

"Yes providing you don't tell me Norfolk jokes. Do you have brothers or sisters?"

"Yes one of each, brother is a farmer now and sister a nurse; she's good at hand holding."

"Do you see much of them?"

"Not often at present, but we try to get together for special birthdays and Christmas. I've been pretty well occupied with work, travel, and a steamy affair, which by the way is over and she is back in Australia."

We were both quiet for a while, then she suddenly said. "Let's finish the champers and walk a bit, I would like to paddle in the sea."

"OK by me, your wish is my command." She smiled at that.

We wandered down to the front, stepped down a walkway where there was a bar and a few seats, plus some loungers down by the water's edge. Even though it was now approaching late evening, we took two side by side, within a minute were approached by a smiling waiter asking what we wanted.

"Champagne again?"

"Yes I can just about manage one more glass."

The beach was very stony where we were, the water gently lapping on the edge of them. I was completely at ease with Maria, and didn't feel it necessary to carry on a conversation. I'm sure she felt the same because she appeared to be deep in thought, gazing at the sea. I wondered where this was leading. It was certainly intriguing and I wondered again about the dark glasses. Was she keeping her features hidden, and if so why?

The champagne arrived with some olives, we picked at them, and she suddenly stood up and said, "I want to put my feet in the water."

"Are they conditioned?" I asked, "as the stones will be uncomfortable."

"I can take that," she said, took off her shoes and walked slowly to the sea. I wasn't filled with the same desire and sat and watched her wander along the edge of the sea. She appeared to be well balanced on the stones; she turned back after about fifty yards and came slowly back to our beds.

The waiter meanwhile was removing the few beds that were alongside us. "Will you be wanting any more champagne?" he asked in very good English, "I will be closing the bar in a little while."

"No, we are fine thanks," and I asked him for the bill.

"Do you have a handkerchief?" Maria asked, "I would like to dry my feet."

"It's pretty grubby, let me see if I can magic one up from the waiter." I went up to the little bar where two women were slagging off someone, the waiter was trying to ignore them.

"Do you have a small towel or anything that my friend can dry her feet with?"

He put on the broad smile again and dipped behind the

bar, coming up with a small white towel with a plastic hook on it. "She can have this and you can also have your bill." I thanked him and took both things with me, I was a bit horrified by the champagne cost, but I had guessed it would be steep there.

She dried her feet and then said "I thought an English Sir Galahad would have offered to dry them for me."

"I thought about it, was tempted, but I fell short. Is this the end for me? in fact it would have been an outstanding thing to have done, and then I would have swept you into my arms and walked into the sea singing, *'I've just met a girl called Maria'.*"

"Oh that old thing again."

"Maria. It would have given me great pleasure to have held you even for a moment or two, but, you did say let's keep it as friends." I twisted the champagne glass in my hand and drained it. "What if I fall for you? What if I'm tempted to plant a kiss or hold your hand and nuzzle a finger or two? Us Norfolkers are romantic I believe, when the tide's in."

She smiled. "Hold my hand, its cold from the champagne, warm it with your Norfolk passion, but that's as far as it should go."

A great sloppy dog suddenly came lolloping down to the sea, eyed us speculatively I wondered if he liked olives and held one out to him, He was a splendid boxer all muscle and sinew. He came up and licked the olive from my hand, pulled a face and galloped off.

"He knew when to leave," she said. "He must have sensed you were getting romantic. It's the champagne, we've been tippling much of the day, what say we call in at a crepe restaurant and I will treat you to one of your choice."

"That's a great idea."

We got up and the waiter collected his money from the little plate on the table beside our beds, and smiling told us we would be welcome any day, he would reserve the best beds for us tomorrow. I thanked him and said, "Maybe."

We wandered back towards our hotel and just at the edge of the old town we saw tables and chairs outside a crêperie, we sat side by side looking out towards the sea and I slipped my hand into hers, she squeezed it and held it,

"That's a bit forward," she smiled.

"It's the thought of a crêpe that's given me courage."

"Better not buy you a steak then, or oysters."

We ordered, we ate, we both drank water, we talked, the evening sun disappeared, and we both knew that it would be tempting to spend a night together.

She was still wearing her dark glasses and I wondered if they were permanent. We eventually got up from the table after she had treated me to a superb crêpe, and walked slowly back to the hotel. I asked at reception if there were any messages, no one wanted me. Riding up in the lift I said, "I could check if the settee in the sitting room made into a bed, and if they had sheets and blankets in the room." She didn't react to that.

When we went in, I flopped down and she asked if we had any music. "Dunno, have a look around, I've just got a bit of work to do, check over my equipment and such. I would also just like to see the news, I believe we can get BBC from here."

"Do you really want to watch the news?" she came over and sat beside me. "I would rather talk, let's make the most of this glorious room," and she grasped my hand twisting my little finger back.

"Oh you brute." I said, and put my arm around her, we hugged she turned up her face to me and I kissed her gently, she responded and we stayed like that for some minutes.

She then said "I'm getting prepared for bed, will you sleep in this room or shall I? Let's look out sheets," and she started opening cupboards and with a triumphant yell, said. "Here's everything you need. Sheets, duvet, blankets; lets pull out the bed."

After some struggling we made it, and she then made it up. I was a staring zombie by then. Why didn't she want me to see the news, surely the BBC wouldn't be too much to follow. I was getting a bit manic, I wonder why she left Paris so quickly, without any plans for staying anywhere. No that's too much to worry about, she's fine, she's been easy and interesting, it would be more interesting to share her bed but, I had started this by saying friends. Friends! I must be losing it. She's beautiful, she just responded to my kiss, why am I getting paranoid? Maybe, just maybe, she might find her way to my bed in the night, the thought aroused me, no, control boyo.

She had taken one of the dressing gowns from the bathroom and swept in, sunglasses off, she was beautiful, maybe slightly older than I had first estimated, but, even with a face now devoid of makeup she was very attractive and I told her so. "My golly you scrub up well."

"That's the second flattering statement today. Are you trying to get intimate Alan?"

"Could be but, I overdid the friendship thing don't you think, looking at you without the glasses is like seeing a vision that's been sheltered under a beautiful tree."

"That's a lovely thing to say, why don't you get ready for bed, so you will be up with the sparrows in the morning."

"Don't you mean larks? I don't have to be at the site until nine so we could have breakfast together, then if you wanted to come to the shoot, you would be welcome."

"Let's see, I like my bed so if I'm awake I may just do that," she came up to me and kissing me on the cheek said. "Thank you Alan, I have really enjoyed my time with you. You have no idea what chaos I was in when I climbed into the train, not knowing where I was going, why, and what the outcome would be."

"Tell me" I said, "why was it chaos? Why did you leave suddenly, are you in some sort of trouble?"

"I will tell you all tomorrow, let's have a quiet night out at dinner if you are not too needed by a horde of glamorous models. Will there be models draped over the cars?"

"I've no idea, I will be told what they want by the producer and that is what I shall do. If any beautiful French model asks me out, I shall politely refuse saying I am spoken for...Ha... What do think of that?"

"Very touching, I may just relax and sit on the balcony with a book maybe, or get out to speak a bit of French, so far I've been speaking English and am missing the verbs."

"Get yourself a key card then, I am on the front initially near the Negresco hotel, then we shall retire to a studio I guess. Have you got a mobile? then I can keep you up to date with where I am."

"I have but the battery is flat, I will get it topped up during the day. Don't bother to call me unless you are going to be very late. Then leave a message at reception with your number and I will venture out to you."

With that she said goodnight and went into the bedroom closing the door firmly. I went into the bathroom and then decided to watch the news, see what was happening,

I looked into the Hotel services book and saw yes, they have BBC1 and 2, I switched on, the time in England was just 10pm, I kept the volume low and the news came on with the lovely Fiona Bruce trying to stare down two or three million people, as she delivered her information. More upsets in Afghanistan, Prime Minister trying to bring forward deployment there, The Olympics building up, some trouble with ticketing, rain needed in East Anglia. I thought about my home village, never thought that could happen there, a hose ban. Stock market floundering as the euro wobbled, all pretty dull stuff. Fiona let her gaze settle on me and the many other admirers, she introduced reporters from different parts of the world. I was just about to switch off when she said French Police still holed up in the east end of Paris, trying to calm some French rebels who are demonstrating about the removal of a politician, whose wife has gone missing after trying to slay him with a sword... No pictures, then the local news came on and I switched off. Well, I can get a paper in the morning and catch up with it all, I telephoned down and asked if I could order un times, "yes," the gruff receptionist said, "but it won't get to us until about 9.30, shall I hold it here or deliver to your room?"

"Hold it please."

I got myself ready for bed, took out my book and tried to read a bit, my mind wouldn't settle, Is there anything I can do to get her to tell me why she is running from something. I thought of knocking at her door and offering myself with some comfort but, she had seemed adamant that it was to be a friend's situation.

I woke with a start the dawn was just showing, I looked at my wrist watch, 6.58. I turned over and tried to sleep, but eventually got up, shaved and made myself beautiful for the day.

It was now 7.40, I thought I would go down to breakfast, I scribbled a note to Maria to the effect that's where I would be for the next half hour or so.

I was about to sit down in the breakfast room when I noticed that the man on the next table to me had his newspaper, *Le Monde*, lying on the chair beside him. On the front page was a photo of a man and woman, my heart rate quickened, as the woman looked a bit like Maria. I went to reception and asked if I could have a copy of the same newspaper which she booked to my room and handed it over.

I sat in an easy chair near reception, all thoughts of breakfast gone. It was Maria, except her name was Claire, English wife of politician disappears after trying to run him through with a ceremonial sword, which he had as a souvenir of past days in the army. He was recovering in hospital, but, she was gone from Paris. Some students causing a fuss about the politician, and the police were wanting to question her as to what had caused the marital fight.

I read the whole article, well as much as my limited French would allow. My mind raced, would I be charged with concealing a criminal? How come no one here had noticed her, but then she did wear the sun glasses all the time, so that was the reason, She would confess, that was all she had said last night, eight o'clock perhaps she will want to sit on the balcony for breakfast, as there was no doubt she would be noticed now if she appeared in Nice.

I went back to my suite, knocked on her door and said, "Maria we must talk", after some minutes she appeared looking very tired. "Did you sleep?" I asked,

"Not very well, I had many things on my mind."

"I know Claire, you must have."

She started. "What do you mean?"

"Claire, I have seen a newspaper, and I now realise why you were running. Look you are on the front page of the paper." I held it up for her, she took the paper and sat down on my bed.

"I'm sorry, I should have told you. It was purely accidental, I discovered he was having an affair and I picked up the sword just to warn him, I was furious with him. I had no intention of using it but he suddenly tried to wrestle it from me, and, during the pulling and pushing it somehow cut him in the side. I panicked and ran from the apartment, called the ambulance service on my mobile, and without a second thought went to the train station to get away somewhere. The rest you know. I will give myself up today and face the music."

"You had time to get your small bag," I suggested.

"Yes we women always carry bags. You've seen what I have in it, I grabbed it as I ran."

I looked seriously at her. "What will you say to the gendarmerie, you need to be careful what you tell them. Why are the students getting upset with your husband. What has he done to cause that?"

"Some of his policies are hurtful for the youth of France, he is seen as a hard right man, and for some time now he has been under pressure from the left. He has also said, send back all the refugees to their countries. We don't want them here. This little episode has given them reason to increase their unrest."

"I don't understand, have they tried to illicit sympathy from you? Obviously you could have some influence on him."

"Alan, I understand your concern, but please don't get involved. I made a mistake running away, you have been most kind to me and have helped me but, I must face up to what I have done and return to Paris." She smiled. "I must say I was tempted to come to your bed last night and on two occasions as I was lying awake I nearly did."

"Would that have been getting your own back on your husband?"

"No you are very attractive, and it would have been easy."

"I nearly knocked at your door," I said. "This sounds a bit old fashioned but, as we both made a thing about friendship, I resisted, and laid awake thinking about it. You could stay here probably on the balcony for the day, and we could catch up tonight."

"It's tempting but I must do the right thing. I will leave

you my mobile number, not my house number and please call me when you finish this job. If you are coming through Paris, stay overnight. I will let you know of a hotel near to where I live. If I'm not in jail," she smiled. "I will be pleased to see you."

"Thanks, I hope this trouble will soon clear up for you. I've enjoyed your company very much and would love to see you in Paris."

"Go have your breakfast and I will hand in my key card when I leave," she stepped forward and kissed me hard on the lips.

I put my arms round her and whispered. "Save some for me in two or three days time." I disentangled myself from her and left the paper on the bed, turned round as I opened the door and said. "Its been a memorable day." blew her a kiss and softly closed the door. Phew, I slipped down the stairs, didn't want to ride in the lift with anyone and went back to the breakfast room.

I thought about the situation for her as I covered my croissant with apricot jam. Was she telling me all? Why would students rise up against a politician because of his right wing views? There must be more to that. I should have kept the paper. I was about to get up from my table when the three commercial guys walked in.

"Hi Alan," said Kevin the director, "you're looking like you've lost a pound and found a penny." He was Australian, tall dark haired and now with a small beard adorning his face. He had made a reputation for commercials with Ford and Volvo,

The other two, Peter and Simon, both stretched out their hands to me, Simon grumbled about cheap flights leaving at 5am. I'll need to be in bed by seven tonight unless you've laid on some totty.

"No chance of that, I've been closely watched yesterday

and this morning, had no time to socialise with totty here yet."

"Oh who watched you then?" said Simon. I thought of telling them the story but decided it would keep. They wouldn't believe me anyway.

"We will book in then maybe meet you down here in half an hour for breakfast."

"Ok I can eat another croissant meanwhile I have a little puzzle to unravel."

They stormed off to reception, I quietly went back to my room, as I entered the phone was ringing, I thought, Ah she's changed her mind, I picked it up.

"Alan Sears?"

"Yes."

Deep man's voice. "Meet me on the left hand side of reception in 10 minutes."

"Who are you, what do you want?"

"I will be standing there wearing a brown cashmere jacket with a brown man's bag over my shoulder."

"I have no interest in meeting you…"

"You will when we have met."

"I don't think so."

"If you value your recent companion, be there," and he hung up.

I checked that I had all my equipment, picked up my bag, must be ready for the day, got the lift and went down, came out of the lift and started walking towards reception when I see two gendarmes leading a man in brown jacket and bag over his shoulder towards the exit doors. He is pulling at their arms and frantically looking around the hotel. I stand very still and watch them disappear. Then I realised he was on the pavement looking at us last night as we walked out.

CHAPTER 2

I stood stock still for maybe a couple of minutes. Should I go back to my room and tell Maria what had happened? I preferred the name Maria. Then I wandered up to reception and asked in my best French, "What's that all about?"

"Don't know monsieur," said the receptionist. "The gendarmes arrived a few minutes ago, went straight to him and then led him out. Not seen him here before."

I thanked her and sat down near a huge bouquet of flowers. This was intriguing. Had she been followed from Paris. Had she been recognised, was he a journalist, or something more sinister? I was about to go to my room to talk to her when Kevin arrived looking slightly the worse for wear.

"What's up doc?" he said, "you look like you've seen a ghost."

"Maybe I have," I replied, "in fact I think I may have been set up as a willing accomplice for a heist of magnificent proportions."

"Hey that's deep. Want to tell me about it?"

"Not really, I've been trying to work out how I could have been brought into something, or was it just a coincidence that I met someone who seems to be somewhat shady."

"Not with you doc."

"Well yesterday I met this very attractive lady on the train down, and it developed a bit to her staying with me, in separate rooms I might add, and just a few minutes ago someone told me on the phone her life may be in danger, and I was to meet him, but, during the time it took me to get down here, he was nabbed by the police and led away."

"Phew is this your next thriller?"

"I'm serious."

"Is that it?"

"No, she's the wife of a French politician, and she tried to run him through with a sword, then beat it. But she's going back today apparently, to face the music."

"Leave well alone I suggest."

"Intriguing though, don't you think?"

We wandered into the breakfast room and it was the usual buffet. Where have the hotels that serve you breakfast gone. We helped ourselves to breakfast. Kevin was definitely the worse for wear, and he drank copious amounts of black coffee to revive himself. Then the other two came in, they both wanted to know what time we were meant to be on the shoot. "I'm ready to go," says Kevin. "I'll get set up by the time you two slugs get there, are you coming as well Alan?"

"Yep may as well, hang on a minute, just remembered something in my room." I went up by lift opened the door and heard voices coming from her bedroom, I pushed open the door and she was on her mobile and talking in a language I couldn't place. She saw me and muttered a good bye I guessed, and turned to me, "What's that all about I asked?"

"Oh I was talking to our Finnish housekeeper, telling her that I would be back today." I was tempted to suggest she had said that the battery was down on her mobile, but kept it to myself.

"I just wanted a last look at you Maria, and I need to

leave." She almost ran at me and kissed me hard on the lips, then whispered. "Please see me in Paris."

"OK."

I left her with a last lingering look then met Kevin and followed him out to a taxi, it was no distance to The Negresco, but we collectively had a fair amount of equipment.

"Better get the rest of my equipment" said Kevin, "it's at reception in the porters lodge. Will you give me a bit of a lift?"

"Well I have my own, so hope it's not very heavy. Wouldn't it be better to get the other two to bring most of the gear?"

The day passed for me in a haze, whilst I concentrated on the work in hand my mind was trying to decipher what could have caused the interruption of the man I was to meet. Who was he? now probably lying in some cell. Why did she lie about her mobile, what was the language she was using when I walked into the suite? I had Maria's telephone number, I wondered if it was genuine.

We finished for the day and we all came back together and decided to meet up later, and have dinner at a restaurant that a friend of Kevin's had recommended. When I got to my suite there was a sealed letter on the coffee table. My pulse quickened as I tore it open.

Dear Alan, you are probably by now wondering what you have got yourself into with me. I heard from the receptionist that a man who had been asking at the desk which room you were in, had been taken away by the police. I've no idea who it could be but, with the vigilance of the press nowadays, one can never be too careful. I can only think that he was interested in a story about me-us, I suppose that being who I am, and having disappeared, there will be press people particularly on the lookout. I doubt if any of the government secret organisations are involved, but that will be short lived as I am travelling back soon to face the music. No doubt you will read in tomorrow's papers that I am in circulation again, and there will be many a surmise as to what really happened. But, you have my telephone number, when you come back through Paris, please call me, and if I'm not incarcerated I will be very pleased to see you. Thanks again for your friendship and concern.

'Maria.' Xxx

I sat down and read through the note twice more. I was mystified about the whole occasion, and wondered if it would be wise to ignore the last bit of the letter, and not stop on my way back. I suppose I should wait to see if anything has been written about her in the papers tomorrow, but, I wonder who the character was that the police led away. I had a shower then turned on the news to see if anything had happened that might relate to Maria, but no mention at all. Maybe it was all being hushed up. I took a gin and tonic from the mini bar and slowly dressed. May as well make the most of my luxury whilst here.

When I went down to the bar Kevin was already there with a large glass of beer nestling on the bar, "What ho cobber, what do you want? the others will be down in a jiffy. What did you make of the presentation today?"

"I thought it went very well, also liked the model displayed over the bonnet, we should have asked her out tonight, you could have shown her your tattoos."

"Jealous huh," he smiled. "She did seem to fancy me a bit, but then most of them do."

"In your dreams."

"Right, we are going to the *Petite Jardin* restaurant, apparently it's the ex-presidents favourite, and Elton John goes there whenever in town, so we might load the expenses a bit."

"Sounds good, just had a G&T from the mini bar, so another one might just get me juices flowing, where is the restaurant?"

"Towards the old town, we can get a taxi there, then maybe walk back through the warm dark evening holding hands!"

"You sound as if you're writing the script?"

"I wasn't too impressed with the words today about the car, were you?"

"They slipped by me but, I would rather have the model for a fast ride around town!"

"Keep your dirty mind out of it."

"Hey you two, deep in love talk?" The other two arrived.

"What's your tipple?" asked Kevin. They both wanted G&T's.

We then went outside the hotel, there were three taxis on the stand, we took the first. The restaurant was packed, but they had one large round table just inside the door vacant, which we were offered. This will help with the expenses we all agreed, but the food was sensational.

"I can see why the president likes it," mutters Kevin, "some real totty here too."

I was lost in thought, I wonder what will be the outcome of my day yesterday? I decided I would call when I got to Paris, and see where that leads. We finished our meal and wandered back along the front, I was ready for bed. I'd not slept too well last night and the soft pillows called. I wished the others good night; they were carrying on drinking at the hotel bar.

Next morning I hurried down to reception and asked for my newspaper. During breakfast I scanned it rapidly but, no mention of Maria. That left me worried, was she alright, had she been dealt with? Surely after the TV programme she must be news, or at least her husband should be. I was about to get back in the lift when two men stopped in front of me and one asked in English if I had a few minutes as they were concerned for my welfare.

"I'm sorry, what do you mean, you're concerned, why is that, and who are you?"

"We know that you spent some time yesterday with a lady from Paris, and we wondered what your connection was?"

"I'm sorry, but I don't think I need to tell you any of my news, nor do I need to answer anything. In fact, I very soon have to start work, and I need to visit my room before I go."

The taller one of the two pulled out an identification card showing a photo of himself, and said. "Look at this, you can talk here or at our station." He was a Superintendent Gendarme.

"Let's sit somewhere" he said, so we went to a deserted corner and pulled up three chairs.

"Why am I being questioned?" I asked.

"Because the lady in question is under surveillance, and you spent a great deal of your time in her company, that's why."

"Yes, but why is she under surveillance? She seems perfectly harmless to me."

"She was the subject of a newspaper report yesterday, she has been apprehended on her arrival in Paris and questioned."

"I think you have got what we say in England, a red herring."

The superintendent said. "What has a red herring got to

do with your relationship with this lady?" I almost smiled, so he could speak good English but, was out of touch with our easy references.

"Let me explain." I then told them the complete story of our meeting and subsequent time together, even saying she had told me her name was Maria, which I believed until I saw the paper. I just had a friendly day with her, the only initial thing that concerned me was the fact she wore sunglasses most of the time, until much later in the suite after she had a shower.

They both seemed to be content with my explanation, and the superintendent said, "Where will you be if we need to contact you?"

"I may have another day or two on a photographic shoot, that depends on the producer. Last night he seemed content, but we shall know in the next hour or so, otherwise I will be here in the hotel. If I'm not wanted, I will catch a train back to England as soon as possible."

"We will need a contact number or address for you in England." I gave them my address and then added.

"My work takes me all over the world, I am never in London for very long."

"That's alright," the superintendent said. We believe what you have told us, I would suggest that on no account should you try to contact your Maria."

"You needn't worry about that, obviously I was led easily into this affair, and I shall most certainly avoid any further contact." Even as I said this, I know my curiosity was heightened, but there is no doubt a major operation going on, so I must keep my word. They thanked me and left me wondering what to do next. I went to my room, sat and puzzled; what could she be involved with that caused police in Nice to want to interview me, and, if she was more important, was her husband also involved. Was his affair excuse just a cover up, could I believe her story? I resolved to see if I could in any way get to the bottom of this. I would telephone her when I got to Paris, but buy a throwaway mobile, so as to have no identification problems. I have read quite a few detective novels, so I thought I would be up to a bit of subterfuge, and, it was a slice of excitement. I went down to the reception and asked for the film crew."

"They are in the front area of the hotel, you will find them there."

I went into the glassed off area that was also a restaurant, they were sitting round a table with a stack of croissants in the centre, a large coffee pot and baguettes.

"Just having your brekky you lot, any news on the car. Are we needed?"

"Nothing as yet," mumbled Kevin, his mouth full of croissant. After a little time of discussing yesterday's work, we were duly summoned back to the studio, there was some tidying up to do, particularly with the commercial, but they also wanted me there for some extra stills. We took two taxis and I spent a long day retaking much of what we had done the day before, but, late afternoon the producer was content and thanked us all, said he would be in touch regarding our payment. We all trooped back to the hotel.

It was too late to get a train to Paris, and we had another evening together in an Italian restaurant and eventually, after some cognac at the hotel, I staggered off to bed. It took me some time to get to sleep but, I determined to call her when I was in Paris, to see if there was anything I should know.

I was having a leisurely breakfast when Kevin surfaced, as we talked he offered me work in Serbia where he was due in three weeks time. That set the seal on a good relationship, extra work and more travel; can I drive to Serbia? I wondered.

CHAPTER 3

I caught my train and whiled away some time looking at the work I had on camera. I also wrote a letter to Maria, just in case I chickened out of meeting her. I wasn't sure if I really wanted to, following the warning from the Gendarmerie. Then I decided to have some lunch, went to the dining car and unlike my journey down there were a few tables left. I went to the end one and sat down. I had just ordered my lunch with a Leffe beer when a man came up to the table and said. "Do you mind if I join you?"

I looked around, there was still three empty tables. "Why join me when there are others not being used?" I said.

"Because Mr Sears I have news for you." I stared at him open mouthed, somewhat shocked at the introduction, and managed to stammer, "how do you know my name?"

"We have kept an eye on you since we first discovered you were with the lady when you arrived."

"Who are you?" I asked.

"You had a meeting with our superintendent and I am following up. I have things I want to discuss, I'm pleased you came to the end table, as we are reasonably sheltered from anyone overhearing what I have to say." I realised he was talking in perfect English, as had been his superior.

"I don't know why you think I can help you in any way. I told your men the complete story of my association, and I object to you thinking I can be of further use. I suggest you leave me. I got the message not to see her when I went through Paris and I have no intention of doing so."

"Please Mr Sears, I have another angle to discuss, perhaps I can give you more reason to listen to me. Your lady is under observation, as is her husband, who you know is a minor player in the French Government. They are suspected of trafficking refugees we want to prove that, and at the same time arrest the middlemen and perpetrators, who are dealing with them at source. After some discussion we would like to make you an offer to assist us, which will mean we now want you to meet up with her, and see if you can get any leads on their activity. Would that be of interest to you?"

I thought about this and realised I knew nothing of how to dig for information. I had an experience recently of someone that had been involved with S.O.E. and he had amused and interested me with some of his stories, but, did I want exposure to the secret services of our country, or France?

"I don't think I can be of use to you, I know nothing of spy work other than having read many a novel, and I like reading Stella Rimmington, But I doubt if I can be helpful to you."

"Well we think you can, and I'm sure you would be interested in seeing her again."

I thought about this and then it struck me. Of course I would like to see her again, and if I didn't have any worries about the outcome, I should enjoy it.

"Yes I will see her again, but I can't promise that I can discover anything about her involvement with refugees."

"Thank you Mr Sears, now this is what I would like to propose."

CHAPTER 4

Sometime later the train pulled into the station. I casually glanced around to see if anyone was taking a particular interest in me, but there were so many people hurrying towards the exit that it was pointless. I thought I would buy a cheap phone, get to a restaurant and then telephone her, and, when I leave, watch to see if anyone was tailing me.

She answered on the third ring and as I started to say hello she cut me off immediately and said.

"Oh hello Maria, how are you? Oh you're staying at L'Hotel Principe. Good, how long are you here for. Two days. It's a flying visit is it? Well shall we meet for coffee tomorrow morning; yes, eleven o'clock suits me fine, I look forward to catching up then. Bye." and she was gone. So Maria is the code.

I went outside and hailed a taxi, L'Hotel Principe please, in my best French, a grumbled *oui*, and we were off. It was on the left bank, I enjoyed the journey taking in all I could in the short time it took to reach the hotel and quickly made myself comfortable in an attractive room, settled in for the evening, thought about being a tourist but I just wandered out, and with ease found a restaurant, and treated myself to a delicious dinner.

As I retired to bed I thought, well, I have taken the plunge, what if it's dangerous? It's too late now but will she come to my room, or should I be in the café at the front of the hotel? I decided I would be in the café. After all, eleven o'clock, the cleaners are likely to be in my room at that time. I slept fitfully and at one stage started to read a book I had brought with me, but eventually I saw it was 8.45 got up, showered and went down for breakfast.

Ten forty-five arrived pretty rapidly and I sauntered down to the café. Propping up a newspaper which I had found at reception, I waited, and kept a close look on the road in front of the hotel. A taxi drew up and she leapt out, paid it off and swept into the café. There were only four others there and they have been since I arrived. I watched to see if anyone came near the hotel and were keeping an eye on her, but all seemed to be clear. I got up and gave her a kiss on the cheek. She looked marvellous, the glasses were on as usual as she sat beside me.

"Alan I know it's a risk for you to be seen with me as I am now a notorious criminal, as some would say but, you and I know better. I expect you were warned off me by the plod at Nice, but that obviously didn't deter you, and here you are in all your glory. How did the shoot go?"

"Let me get you a coffee. Anything with it?"

"No, just black will be fine."

"The shoot went well, I think, and I have been offered work in Serbia. But, tell me your news. Were you arrested when you arrived in Paris? The gendarme said you would be, and what about the sword bit, there must be a whole story now, and I'm all ears. He warned me off seeing you by the way."

"Alan, I have good news and bad news, much as I would like to spend real time with you, I can't. My husband has declared that he wouldn't employ anyone to keep an eye on me but, if I did get close to you in any way, he would have me thrown out of the comparative luxury that I enjoy. But even more hurtful would be a trumped up charge that would see me in jail."

"Wait a minute," I said. "Taking into account the student unrest against your husband, your dash for freedom, threatening behaviour by him, what is going on? How are you implicated in anything that would be seen as anti-establishment?"

"Alan, I will try to explain. At the moment in France we have a great many refugees, many of them wanting to stay in the country, others desperate to get to your country. He has stated officially that they are not welcome in France, and, if he had his way he would round them up and export them back to their own countries. That has been disowned by the government. They say he has taken a personal view, we as a nation cannot begin to arrange this, consequently he has created many enemies. But, to the real point. He has said that his affair was over, it wasn't anything to be worried about, and he was entirely happy with me in all respects."

"But are you, Maria? Are you happy that he let you down in terms of marriage and loyalty. It must have hit you hard to make you leave and take a train to anywhere?"

"Yes and I thank you again for helping me get over my recklessness, but, I think my priorities are to be loyal to him and, the French see life in a very different way to the English. It's almost common knowledge that many of our men in high positions have mistresses."

"Maria, you were definitely very upset when I first met you, I think his threats are superficial. You know and I know, we could be very good for each other. I missed you very much after you had gone, we had enjoyed some magical moments and I would love to get even closer to you. I'm sure you could make excuses to your husband to spend time with me, your friend Maria!! Even if not here in Paris, perhaps you could visit me in London."

"Alan I would love too but I'm afraid of the consequences."

"Which are they, treatment from your husband or falling in love with me?"

"I know I could, and yes I would love to spend time with you. The daytime here is not the best to pursue that, I will see if I can get away later today and meet in your room."

"I would love that but what if your husband gets tied into the refugee situation, would that mean him going to Calais perhaps, or any other place where they are congregating?"

"I don't think he will be needed to actually visit them publically, but he does travel quite a lot and he may well be going to the Middle East again. He has had to follow up various programmes in Turkey of late, or so he told me. I can let you know his diary, and then we can meet, but today, I will get back and see if he is tied into any meetings or travel and call you, then perhaps we might get some time together."

"I'm prepared to wait a day or so but let me know as soon as you can. I've seen every statue and exhibition in Paris during my visits so let's meet up this evening if possible, and I will let you into a secret."

"Oh lovely, I love secrets. I will call as soon as I can," with that she stood up and swept out. Phew, I didn't get very much other than the fact her husband visits the Middle East and Turkey. What will they make of that?

I got out the card my train spotter had given me and called his number.

"I have seen her."

"Yes we know, did you get anything of importance?"

"Very little other than her husband visits the Middle East fairly often, and Turkey, don't know if that helps?"

"Yes it does, that ties in with our information, we need to

know where he goes in Turkey. Are you seeing her any more today or while you are here?"

"I'm waiting for her to call."

"Well done Mr Sears, we may hire you on a regular basis if you can derive news for us."

I thought that I had easily been led into something that had always fascinated me, cloak and dagger stuff. On one job that I did in Finland I had met a very charming highly intelligent man, whom I had helped with a car, which had developed a puncture. He had no idea of how to change to his spare – unless of course, being very bright, he didn't want to get his hands dirty – and me – I was taken in. So I changed his wheel for him and he invited me to his hotel for a drink, which I gladly accepted. Whilst mopping up two bottles of Chablis, he confided in me a bit after he realised I was just a Brit photographer on a job, photographing some farm machinery, telling me that he was a diplomat, and headed up a small office in the country. He made a joke that he sat on his office roof garden with a pair of binoculars and watched Russia, to see if anything underhand was going on. That was about as far as he would go, but I know the term diplomat carries some mystique, because that is what I understand to read spook. I enjoyed his company and he was obviously able to soak up the alcohol, as he said he had an embassy dinner to go to, and that meant slurping for some hours. I gave him my card and said if ever he wanted a wheel changed, to give me a call.

CHAPTER 5

I settled into my hotel room and started to read my book when the telephone rang, it was Maria. Yes, her husband had a call to go to Calais. He had to make some decisions regarding the migrants there. I asked him what the decisions would be, but he said it was too early to give any indication of what he had to do. And, he's staying overnight. Would you be up to entertaining me with either a take-away or room service?

I said I was an expert in room service, she laughed and said. "Calm down tiger...I will be with you in an hour or so, what is your room number?"

I gave it to her and immediately started tidying my room. This was exciting. I wonder if her husband is just trying her out and will keep a watch on her movements. It was too late to let that worry me, I cleaned my teeth, had a quick glance at myself in the mirror to see if there was anything I should do, and then looked at the hotel book of services. They had a pretty good choice of food and a wide variety of wines. That's that then I thought. All I want is some courage to deal with my potential fun.

A knock at the door, "Yes."

"It's me, Maria." I quickly opened the door, bowed

slightly and said. "Please come in to my delightful sexy home."

She was wearing her sunglasses again, and was dressed in the most beautiful slacks and light green silk top, which did her body the power of good. I gulped and stared at her, then stepped forward and put my arms round her. I pressed my face to hers, we stood like that for what seemed ages. I leant back and went to kiss her, she slipped out of my arms and said. "Not yet Alan, let's talk. I have much to tell you and am a little breathless from hurrying up the stairs. Didn't dare use the lift."

"Let's sit." We sat side by side on the settee, I held her hand and waited for her to speak.

"Life is very difficult at the moment, I know my husband is wanting to know just what happened between us, as he has had some briefing I believe from the police in Nice."

"I told them the truth of what had happened and they seemed ok with that."

"Yes, but I also think that one of our secret services has taken an interest in me, can't think why as I'm, as you know, a simple soul."

I didn't dare tell her that I had been asked to see her and try to discover if her husband was involved in anything that could be seen as detrimental to France.

"Is your husband at home with you now, obviously he has to attend any government meetings but how is your relationship. Are you on good terms, or are things difficult between you?"

"We are not sleeping together if that's your real question. In fact, I think it's going to take some time to repair our relationship if at all." She seemed a little sad when she finished that sentence. My heart went out to her. Although I was very attracted to her, I also felt sympathy for her situation.

"I didn't even ask you if you would like anything, tea coffee or a drink?"

She looked very tired just then and I wondered how much this whole episode was affecting her.

"I would love a drink, I know it's just about time over the yardarm, but what do you have in that little fridge?"

"Well it's not very well stocked but, I can summon up a refreshing glass of champers as I have a half bottle."

"That would be most welcome."

"What are your plans?" I asked. "Have you got freedom to spend time with me and will you need to keep out of the public eye?"

"Public eye, that's a good one, I'm not too well known in Paris, but I do wear my sun glasses a lot to keep off hordes of fans wanting to touch me, usually randy old English photographers!"

"That's more like you," I said, "I was worried that your trip to Nice and its after-burn was affecting your sense of humour."

I handed her a glass of champagne, got my own and sat down beside her again. "Can you have dinner with me tonight?"

"I am yours for the evening, won't be able to stay but, let's say in an hour you order room service and we indulge in something sweet and manageable, I will hide in the bathroom when its delivered."

My heart leapt, she is offering herself to me, I was immediately aroused and went to kiss her, she slowly put up a hand and said, "Don't expect too much Alan, I am a bit emotionally frail at present and I don't want you to be upset in how we manage our feelings in any intimacy."

I pulled her towards me and was about to kiss her when the telephone rang, I sat back and tried to calm my nerves, who would ring me? No one knows I'm here except Maria.

"Take it Alan," she said.

I went over to the telephone and picked it up. "Hello."

"Ah bonjour monsieur this is reception and I have a call for your friend that is with you."

How did they know she was here? I thought.

"Sorry but what do you mean my friend?"

"Monsieur I have been told that you have a visitor and the person on the telephone is most insistent that she speaks with them."

"Wait a moment." I put my hand over the mouthpiece and asked her, "Maria, that's reception and they said the caller knew you were here, and she wants to speak with you."

"Did they say who it was?"

"No shall I ask?"

"Yes, it may be my housemaid, she knew I was seeing you?"

"Search me I will see." I held up the phone." Who is that wants to talk to my friend?"

"I will ask Monsieur."

He came back a few seconds later. "It's Madame Lazell Monsieur."

"Wait a moment." I repeated the name to Maria.

"Oh that's ok then, I will take her."

She held the phone very close to her ear and said, "Bonjour Elaine." Then she started talking in Finnish I guess, as it was totally unrecognisable. "Thank you for letting me know," in French. I was a little uncertain if I had heard correctly?"

She listened for a few more seconds and then said. "Thank you I am most grateful. I will be back in half an hour."

She put down the phone and then said, "I'm sorry Alan, but my husband is returning tonight soon so I must go, can I finish my champagne, and can I ask you a small favour."

"Depends how small, I'm already feeling a bit down as I had anticipated spending most of the night with you, and suddenly finding I'm not, has dampened my enthusiasm a bit."

She came up close, put her arms round me, and kissed me, immediately arousing me.

"Alan I had also looked forward to that but, I can't now, and if he is at home, it will be difficult to get away for any length of time."

I stepped back. "What's the small favour then?"

She rummaged in her shoulder bag and drew out an A4 envelope that seemed to be fairly well filled. "I know your studio is in the Victoria area and wondered if you could deliver this for me to the address in Pimlico, I don't trust it to the post office deliveries as it contains some quite valuable fashion designs."

I looked at the address 16 Clarenton St SW1.

"Is that a house or business?" I knew Clarenton Street was mainly houses.

"It's a design centre that I used in my modelling days."

"OK but what about us, can you ever get to London, or is this a goodbye before we really say hello?"

"No it's not goodbye, please leave it to me. I want to, and will see you, just give me a few days to arrange my life, then I will come to London."

She took her last sip of champagne, then said, "I must go Alan, I'm so sorry this has happened but, please understand, things are difficult but I will get over them, and I long to see you when I can be perfectly relaxed." With that she put her bag over her shoulder and kissing me again went to the door. "Don't be too upset, we shall make it." with that went, closing the door softly.

I looked at the envelope, both flaps were bound with a

strong looking tape that ensured they couldn't be steamed open. I wondered what was so important that it had to be personally delivered. I put it down, filled my glass with the remaining champers, and sat down to contemplate what to do. I had booked the hotel for the night so even though I could have caught a late night Eurostar, I decided I would stay.

Is she using me, am I being stupid about this so called relationship. Why would she tell her housemaid where she would be? All those things crept into my reckoning. I thought of opening a small bottle of Chablis that was sitting quietly in the fridge, when the phone went. I grabbed it, had she changed her mind, no it was a man's voice. "I see your friend has gone Alan."

"Who is this?"

"You can call me Harvey. I talked to you earlier on the train about your potential meeting with your friend and wondered, did you get any information? On second thoughts, it would be better if we met in your hotel bar, I don't want to have any recorded messages on the phone, say in ten minutes."

That threw me a bit, how did he know she had left, were they watching me, am I getting in too deep here. Why the secrecy?

I started to pack and then wandered down to the bar, sure enough, there was 'Harvey,' hugging a pint of beer. I thought spy's would drink G and T's but, he greeted me with a handshake and asked what I would like to drink.

"A glass of champers please, I was enjoying one recently in my room until my friend left." The sarcasm passed him by.

"Sure, let's just clear up a few details. What did she tell you about her husband?"

"Well he had to go to Calais and he thought he was going

to stay the night, but her housemaid called to say that he was returning this evening."

"Alan I think you are being used a bit here. He took a flight to Turkey in a private jet, we discovered that, but weren't able to fix to where in Turkey, as it seemed to be a very last minute booking."

"I wondered if this whole episode is a planned affair and I am being used, she asked me to deliver a personal envelope to an address in Pimlico London. She didn't apparently trust the usual mailing companies. And no doubt she thinks I am a besotted admirer and future lover." I said all that with feeling because, if I am being used, when did it start, because our first meeting could not have been planned. Is she somehow involved with her husband in irregularities with the refugee problem, and sees me as a willing dupe?

"The envelope is sealed at both ends so it will be impossible to steam open the flaps."

"Alan I want you to meet someone in the UK that is in my line of business, and he is partly responsible for anything related to the migrant and refugee problem that is hitting our countries. Give him the envelope for an hour or two, perhaps he can get to see what it contains."

"I am wondering if I am being used by your lot as well. I said I was willing to help initially but, this is getting too deep for me, it's already costing me time and money to be here overnight, and if I am seen to be involved by the wrong people, my life could be in danger I suppose."

"At this moment in time you are just helping out, perhaps we can make use of your professional work, as I'm sure our opposite numbers in the UK will also pitch in."

"Yes but how much more will he expect of me? I must say I am very much attracted to my friend and I thought it was reciprocated, until all this news of complicated undercover activity came to light, and as she had apparently fallen out with her husband over an alleged affair, I thought all's fair in love and war."

"Alan in some respects it looks like you are being used by her, but it's only on a peripheral basis, and I wouldn't worry over safety. If she does come to see you in London you will need to ensure that my opposite number there can keep an eye on any untoward activity with either her, or her husband's people. If he is, as we believe, heavily involved in people smuggling in Turkey, or Syria, then large amounts of money are involved. Then it follows that whoever is doing it will be well protected and anyone that could be exposing this should be fearful. I don't at present think you need concern yourself. We obviously have been keeping an eye on you and her, that enabled me to see that she had left you after a very short time, and, I wonder if she had only done it to give you the package to deliver. I know that may hurt your pride a bit, but it's possible. Much will depend on if she does actually come to see you or keep in touch with you, but if not, I would suggest you put it down to a good break whilst you were working here."

"Well thanks for that lecture Harvey. I feel much better now, perhaps I can sleep with only one eye open,"

He smiled. "Alan, don't let all this get to you, just meet my opposite number in the UK and then deliver the envelope to him for an hour or two, you can then relax, and try to forget the whole episode, but, if she does get in touch, let me know and your UK contact, he by the way is Douglas, with MI6. Perhaps MI5 might also get involved if there is much UK work going on. Meanwhile here is my real telephone number, just refer to me in any discussions as Harvey, and thanks for your help so far. I have also given Douglas your telephone number in the UK, so expect a call from him sometime tomorrow."

"I'm going back tomorrow fairly early, I will also be at

my office studio tomorrow afternoon if he wants to contact me. Are our two countries secret services working together on this?"

Yes, we have to be careful of how we approach this, and we hope that perhaps we, and your secret services, can mount an apparent group of film people trying to make a documentary on the plight of refugees. At the same time try to find what the connection is to our man and the financing of them. It would obviously be much better if it appeared to be the UK's initiative, but we would help finance the event. Douglas can give you more background to it.

I relaxed this made sense, but, would they want me involved?

I thanked Harvey and said, "I wish you goodbye and thanks for keeping an eye on me." With that I finished my champagne and went back to my room, packed and decided to eat out, I fancied a galette, *where will I find one of those in chic Paris*?

CHAPTER 6

The next morning after a superb French breakfast, I got a taxi, and three hours later I found myself in home territory. I had kept a wary eye on refugees near the entrance to the tunnel, but all I could see were several riot police lined up along a fence, and very few migrants.

After two hours of checking my mail and emails, calling the agency to talk about the job in Nice, and booking more work in Aberdeen, photographing a new company in decommissioning. That interested me, all my other work there had been for set up, or take over existing fields, by small companies, as the big boys were looking at other sources for their money. But the idea of decommissioning, that was a new one. I knew that every field would have a life expectancy, but is this the new work pattern?

I got a call from Kevin, he had also got back to the UK. "How are you lover boy?" he asked.

"I'm fine Kevin, just a bit jaded after the French visit, but I have learnt a bit this trip. Never be too sure of straight answers."

"What does that mean?" he growled.

"It means I think I was set up a bit there."

"I did suggest you were on delicate ground if you

remember."

"I know, and I didn't take that in, but, now I am happy to be back and have picked up new work in Aberdeen, not certain of the date yet. When I do get back, I'll give you a call and let's get together."

"Urgh" he said. "I'm about to go to the Motor Fair in Berlin, that's a five day job, keep me out of mischief unless I can meet a beauty on a train." With that he snorted a laugh and said. "The Serbia job will now be a month away, I will let you know the dates, see you, all the best."

Almost immediately the phone went again, I picked it up and a voice said, "Hello Alan, I have been asked to call and set up a meeting. My name is Douglas, I presume you know the Ebury Wine Bar, would it be possible to meet there for a drink and maybe a bite this evening?"

"Yes as long as its reasonable early," I replied.

"How would seven o'clock suit you?"

"That's fine Douglas, I will bring the necessary with me. How shall I know you?"

"I will be in the left hand corner of the bar, reading an Evening Standard."

"Thanks, see you there."

Phew that's quick I thought, but I had plenty to do, and it was soon six forty-five, so I brushed my teeth, that always gives me a modicum of health, if I could have taken a shower as well I would have felt better.

It was no distance to the wine bar, and I soon walked in, looked around, there were three couples happily swigging, two men both studying the evening paper. I wondered if either was Douglas, but neither of them looked up as I ordered a gin and tonic. A few minutes later in came a fairly round gentleman in a dark blue suit with a jacket that had a small handkerchief in the top pocket, blue shirt and a striped tie. He came straight to me and shook hands, sat down, introduced himself, and ordered another G&T. That's better I thought, although I always had in my mind any spook should look a bit James Bondy, this one obviously enjoyed his food and drink.

"You've had an interesting time I believe?" he said, lowering his voice.

"Yes you could call it that, certainly well out of my usual comfort zone."

"You may get other opportunities to enjoy some more excitement if this thing is as big as we think, would that be of interest to you?"

"I must say when Harvey first approached me I was a bit enthusiastic, but now, I'm not sure. He did say that it might be dangerous." I was also keeping my voice low. Hey I thought, I'm already a spook, I'm falling into this way of life.

"We are always looking for people that have an inroad to some aspects of life. You have a ready-made contact that could be very useful in getting information in what is an ongoing European problem, that problem is going to get much bigger, we are all assured, but, there are methods of doing this which might be of interest to you to learn. In any event they will always help with negotiations for jobs, work, etc."

"You make it all sound very simple for me but I know it can't be. I've read about drops and holes in walls and seen just about every film made where spies are concerned, and I was a dedicated follower of the BBC 'Spooks' series."

"Weren't we all, that was a riveting series, and not altogether true to life in the service as we know it."

"Let me think things over. If I said I was interested in being a support of some kind, what exactly would it entail?"

"Number one consideration, you would have to sign the Official Secrets Act Form... and that means keeping everything about it to yourself, not even your nearest and dearest can be aware of want level of involvement. Number two, you would have to ascertain how much time you could allocate to the cause, bearing in mind that I am only suggesting this, because you seem to be somehow involved with a person who may well be deeply involved with the smuggling of refugees. You never know what else may creep out of the woodwork, when real money is concerned, many an honest joe has found it attractive enough to forget their upbringing, and parental influence, or education even, when the offer of upgrading the bedroom curtains are a concern. Well make that thicker carpets and a taste of luxury."

"I'm confused, are you suggesting that I could be a sort of runner for you and would be expected to provide information. After all, I may well have been used, or am being used, to pass information via this envelope that I have here. What if it's entirely innocent and she, my so called lady friend, knows nothing of her husband's undercover interests. Wouldn't it be wiser to see if you can screen what is in the envelope and then, perhaps we could have a better understanding of her side of things."

"Yes of course. Harvey informed me of what happened in Paris, and he suspects that she is using you and it was all planned for the so called housemaid to call, after she had been with you for half an hour. She may well have known her husband was flying to Turkey. She may also know that we, with the French, are keeping a watchful eye. The one mysterious aspect of all of this is. Who was the person in Nice that wanted to see you and was led away by the Gendarmes, we have not been able to as yet find out his interests and the French police have methods of extracting information."

He stopped. "Let's eat and I will then see if we can decipher what's in the envelope, and let you know tomorrow.

Meanwhile give all this some thought and perhaps, we will have a clear picture of what to do. We may of course be barking up the wrong tree, and all of our friends activities in Turkey and places are perfectly innocent. The interesting aspect of it all at the present moment is that the French would like us to lead into finding all we can about the financing of the traffickers in Turkey, probably by using a filmed documentary, they don't want to be seen to be associating in it, but behind the scenes they are. This is why you are important to us all."

"Thanks, me, important. I'm in a way flattered but you could say, wary, and I'm ready for some food, I used to eat here fairly regularly, but it's handy for your lot, just cross the river and you're here."

CHAPTER 7

Francios Lazell was sitting quietly in a prison cell in Nice. He had just been questioned for what seemed hours about his involvement with the British photographer and the wife of a politician. He had somehow held out without giving any indication that he had anything that could cause problems, although at times he was close to it. Was he holding back because of fear of reprisals from his own people, even though they were meant to be partners in crime, or did he have evidence about her husband.

His little gang centred around Marseilles. He had been in Turkey two weeks previously near the border with Syria when he, with three other freedom fighters as they called themselves, were on the lookout for any way they could benefit from the hordes of refugees coming in to Turkey. They had hatched up the plot the previous weekend after watching the news about the influx. They were all petty criminals, mainly burglary and some car theft for resale; they hadn't got into drugs, there were three big gangs in Marseilles, and it was common knowledge that they were not concerned with life, and would happily end it for anyone trying to muscle in on their territory. But, they decided that there were gangs already fleecing the refugees in their desperation to get away from the horrors of Syria. Why couldn't they also benefit.

Whilst there they had mixed as much as possible to see if they could pick up anything that could point them in the right direction to start trading with the refugees in escape policies. They had found great difficulty in finding anyone willing to talk about hiring boats, and if they did, where would they be based. Coupled with that, they soon realised that there was a professional body already set up to make the most of the great horde of people that were trying to flee. It was whilst they were trying to get involved they had spent one evening with two hard drinking French ex-soldiers, and one of them, well under the influence, had mentioned that there were some groups that were financed and controlled by high placed French business men, and one of them they believed was a politician who had apparently been seen with some of the people providing shelter, and boats that the refugees could travel in. The two soldiers were boasting about the vast amount of money changing hands, and that they were both better off than they had ever been.

It was at that time that Francois had heard the name mentioned and then he had by chance gone to Nice to see one of his daughters who was being ill-treated by her boyfriend. To such an extent she had sent a text to her father asking him to help and chase off the boyfriend.

Consequently he had arrived at the same time as Alan and Maria and knew it was her from the many publicity photos that he had seen of her at various celebrity events. He wondered why she was with the photographer, and as he found they were sharing a room, had used the telephone call to see if he could involve a little blackmail. Prior to that he had met up with his daughter's boyfriend, and had put the frighteners on him, he felt sure that his daughter needn't worry in the future.

He wondered why the police were so interested in him, was there something really important about the two together, was she involved with any underhand work? Not being too bright he thought he would ask the police that question, why him? when they next continued their questioning. He would also like to contact his friends and see if they had made any progress in getting involved in Turkey.

Clair wrote a letter to her husband, to see when he returned, it could be sometime tomorrow and she wanted him to be aware of what she had done, starting with.

I trust the visit to Turkey was fruitful. The envelope you left for me was being delivered. I'm sure I can trust my man, he is not at all hard-bitten like most photo-journalists, and I know he is very struck with me. I played it well and managed to keep him at arms-length. He is not too persistent and next week you can get over to London and everything should be set up for you. This is all very exciting and, I'm looking forward to seeing the villa you promised in the Seychelles; it will be a good bolt hole for us for years to come. She placed it on his desk in a prominent position.

CHAPTER 8

I was feeling more confident of my security after the meeting and dinner with Douglas, We had analysed my involvement to date. How I could be employed in the future if I wanted that, albeit purely on the question of the French involvement. Douglas had been most forthcoming about the whole situation, having initially ensured that I would be capable of keeping all their discussions to myself. The situation was delicate as they believed some high ranking French people were involved with financing and provision of boats for the refugees. It had to be handled carefully and proven before anyone could be accused. None of the refugees to date had been open with any of the authorities about how they had been approached by the people traffickers. This could be because they might well have relatives that were looking to break away from Syria, and they wanted to keep the channels open, even though it was very expensive to buy one, or more places on the boats taking them to Greece, or Italy. Both the French, and English special services were trying to get the Turkish authorities more involved. They had also approached the German special executives.

Douglas said "We, with our friends are about to send an

independent filming crew to Turkey. The BBC and world news were already involved, but mainly recording the actual boats being landed. Very little as yet had been shown of the start of these perilous journeys, with overloading being the main concern. Would Alan be interested in going with the crew? There would be their own professional film maker, and two of their people, both involved with support for film making. Alan could be part of the crew but, working alongside them as an independent photo-journalist, to see if he could discover any background to the provision of boats. He would be well paid and at all times guarded from any possible attacks."

"This could be of interest," I agreed. "I have many questions as to how I could be involved." I started by asking Douglas...if that was his name. "Initially, surely you would not just hire someone like me on a casual basis?"

"No, I have enquired into your background as soon as Harvey made contact to say that you were being observed by the French. We looked into your business dealings and you are obviously well respected in your line of work, and, following your association with your French lady friend, we would be prepared to enrol you on a one off basis initially, and see if you could become more involved at a later date.

But, at the moment this is a pressing issue and, whilst our prime minister has said that the UK will give a home to twenty thousand refugees, the background to it is more complicated, and we know there are several traffickers already in place here, using a variety of means to get people into the country. Many of them are refugees themselves initially, and are using their knowledge to bring others into the country, through several ports on the continent. We all agree that the real issue is to get to those that are at the sharp end, actually dealing with the masses. Relieving them of anything up to ten thousand pounds each, which multiplied by the hundreds coming, is very big money."

"If I said yes to your proposal, what is the start date, and what training would I need?"

"As far as the work is concerned, you know how to manipulate and record any scenes of people. As far as background training is concerned, you will spend a few days with our training officers in what you would regard as a safe house. As we want to get our team over there as soon as possible, you will need to spend at least a week, and it will entail probably twelve hours a day. What work do you have at present?"

"I have a job in Aberdeen that could be in the next two weeks. I have a possible job in Serbia, but that could be deferred for some time, other than that I could start very soon." I was calm as I said all this but, inwardly very excited. Could I really want to be working as a spook, it was too much to take in but, yes, I would be really tempted to do it.

"Well you decide within twenty four hours, then, we must get going."

"Thanks, I will keep in touch daily and see when the Aberdeen job actually starts. I don't particularly want to hand it on to any of my partners, as I'm sure that decommissioning will soon be a big issue in the oil industry, and, if I am at the front end, it could be a good new line for me."

"Of course you must keep all your normal work going. Here is my card, please keep it safely and call me as soon as you can. I will also let you know if we get any joy from this parcel," which he stuffed into his bag.

I thanked him for his offer and dinner. How would I handle all this? I wanted to go back to my office and start calling my work contacts, but I just settled and went home to my flat in Southwark, made myself a cup of tea and sat down to contemplate the offer.

The next morning after a night of dreams, I quickly had breakfast and caught a taxi to the office, My part time secretary receptionist, Rachel, said I had a few letters, which she had kept to give me on my return, and one call from a man named Harvey yesterday, just after you left. "He didn't leave a message."

"That's ok I have his number." I went into my office and called Harvey.

"You called me," I said when he answered.

"Yes I wondered if you had had any contact from this end and, I believe Douglas is offering you work."

"Yes he has, nothing of importance has happened, if I get any calls I will let you know. I also expect to hear from Douglas soon, as he has the package and they are going to see what can be assessed from their study of it."

"Fine, OK Alan, let's keep in touch."

So he's really calling me Alan now. I called the publicity manager in Aberdeen and asked when I could cover their launch. He said it would be at least a couple of weeks as, no actual date had been fixed as the contractor was having difficulty tying down his client.

So that leaves me free to at least see what sort of training I would get. I called Douglas and told him I could start straight away. "Is it likely to last more than two weeks, my training, and the actual work in Turkey?"

"I can't really answer that Alan; certainly, if we were to start tomorrow, I would expect you to be going to Turkey within seven days but, let's wait. I have the letter under a form of scrutiny and we should have some idea of its contents very shortly. I will set your training in motion and call you with your start time and where. I hope that will be tomorrow."

I told my secretary that I may now be away for at least two weeks. I will have my mobile with me at all times if you need me urgently, but, I would prefer messages in text form as some of the work will be under conditions when it may not work.

"Thanks," she said with a smile, "are you being secretive Alan, you have that look round your mouth when you tell your funny stories, and you've got it now."

Hey I thought, and I am thinking of being a spook, better deal with that.

"What do you mean funny look, and how often do I tell you funny stories?"

"Not often, but you do have a certain twitch to your mouth when you might be telling a fib."

"Well thanks for that, I'd better practice being a hard man."

I took this comment seriously, did I really give myself away. I remember when I used to play poker, one of my best friends said they always knew when I had a good hand because of my mouth. Maybe this whole thing of me being involved with something secretive was a dream, and I would be sensible to just carry on in my photographic life, but, I am intrigued about the set up with Maria, and both the French and British agents, seemingly keen on getting me on board with their work.

I went into the bathroom and had a hard look at myself, twisted my mouth a bit and tried snarling, that didn't impress me, then I tried a knowing look, but that also left me cold. Since school I have been pretty passive, I did box at school and did pretty well, the last fight I had was as a cruiser weight and somehow I had knocked down the one boy at my weight that I really admired. He had been the leading boxer in our class for all the year. I hung up my gloves after that and we became good friends.

I went to my office, sat down, and tried to calculate what I might be letting myself in for. Did I really want to have a week of training in undercover work, if that was what they hinted at. Did I really want to be exposed to danger? I took some time thinking about it, and decided that I had led a pretty sheltered existence since I came to London. Whilst being a photographer had its moments of danger, those moments were usually having to adapt to certain physical placings to get the best angles. I had been very exposed to danger on some jobs, and it had not affected my courage to get the best out of my work. So the answer was yes. I did want to explore this activity, I'm sure it could be very well paid and if they take me on regularly, there are so many problems in the world that the services have to deal with, I'm sure I could be fully employed covering them.

Rachel called and said that a man named Douglas was on the line, did I want to talk to him?

"Yes put him through."

"Alan we need to meet, I have uncovered some intriguing facts from your parcel and I think you need to deliver it a soon as possible."

"Fine can you get it to me."

"Yes and we can talk then. I will see you at the southern end of Eccleston Street where it leads into Buckingham Palace Road, just at the back of Victoria station; say in twenty minutes."

"Yes Ok will see you there."

I quickly finished the report I had started writing with my invoice for the Nice work, told Rachel I would be out of the office for an hour or two, and made my way to our meeting point.

When I met him he said, "In the envelope are instructions to a Maurice Bent to make certain that he had the necessary money to finalise the deal and that her husband would be over in two or three days to complete our end. There was no mention of what the deal involved, other than the fact that her husband had already confirmed that he had arranged flights. So we need to get this to the address, then we can institute watching and tapping their phones. If she intends her husband to be here in a day or two, we have no time to lose, so will you deliver this now? I suggest you try to make contact with whoever is in charge of the house or office. Say that you have been asked to personally deliver this, so you want to ascertain that you are dealing with the right person, and, could they look at the letter and justify my delivering. Also try to get in and see what the set up is."

"Well thanks Douglas, Do you think it required a special delivery, couldn't the post have been ok?"

"Don't know Alan. I think we have seen all that is in the envelope, but I suppose there could be more if certain reflective board or paper is used, but there is certainly a lead there that can be helpful, and we can get our tracking done overnight. See if you notice any security equipment near the entrance door. I know this is all new to you, and your training will help you with observation of this kind, but, it's necessary to get it there, then leave the follow up to us."

"OK will do. Its only ten minutes walk from here, so I will telephone you after I get back to my office with any news."

"Great. I will call you anyway with your address for tomorrow. We have a good safe house in Kent. I think that will be good for you. Our main training place is in Scotland, but you don't need that." and with that he hung up.

I walked quickly through the bus station at Victoria and was soon in Clarenton Street, I found the right number and it looked a substantial house. The ground floor was obviously an office as I could see a lady working at a computer just inside the window. The door was locked I imagine and there was no name of a company on it. I rang the single bell and within seconds a voice asked me what I wanted. I looked at the door but couldn't see a speaker. "I am delivering a letter to your address, it's from a lady in France, there is no name on the envelope just the address."

"Thank you what is your name?"

"Alan Sears."

"Mr Sears we are expecting you," a few seconds later the door was opened by a very trim dark haired lady, she was wearing a very tight skirt which accentuated her very shapely legs. She had on a light coloured pink shirt open at the neck, all in all a welcome sight. She was smiling and thanked me for delivering it. I said, "I'm not sure if it was valuable and I would like some confirmation that I have the right place and person, after all, I was entrusted with this delivery by someone I have recently met. So can you please open your envelope and check that all is correct."

"Please wait here a second or two." We were standing just inside the door and there was a fairly long passage going into the house. "I will get someone for you."

I looked around, there was a barrel type piece of furniture with two umbrellas in it, above that was a wooden coat hanger with several clips and two coats on them. I couldn't see any security equipment at all and, as I was just walking a bit further along the hallway a man came striding up with an outstretched hand and a huge smile on his face. "I'm sorry to keep you Mr Sears. My PA said you wanted confirmation that the envelope you delivered was all in order. Well, I can confirm that it is and I thank you for your concern, that's completely understandable."

"That's OK, can you just confirm who you are, in case my friend in France asks me."

"Yes my name is Maurice Bent, I manage the business here."

"Thanks, what is your business may I ask? this is

obviously a house that you have converted."

"No it's still a house, I have two people working with me and we are a specialist travel company."

"That might be interesting for me as I have a photographic business in Victoria, and do travel a great deal."

"We only deal with two organisations, both associated with governments and we wouldn't have any chance of working for individuals or companies, but thanks for asking, and I wish you well, and thanks again." With that he stepped past me and opened the door.

His hand was out again "Good bye", as I slid past him and started walking back towards my studio I wondered if I had been a bit inquisitive, but he didn't seem to mind that I wanted confirmation and obviously Maria had let them know I was coming. It seemed straightforward, but, I was a bit surprised that there was no name anywhere, either on the wall or the door.

I was only in the studio for a few minutes when the phone went, How did he know I was back? Are they watching I thought. It was Douglas, Rachel said, I picked it up and he straight away asked if it had all gone well?

"I suppose it did," I recalled what had happened and said, "there was no sign of any security but, our Mr Bent did tell me that they were a specialist travel company, only working with governments."

"You met him then?"

"Yes, I demanded to meet someone in authority as I wanted confirmation they had received the envelope in mint condition."

"You didn't use those words did you Alan?"

"No, I just told them I was concerned that I had done the right thing."

"What was your impression of Mr Bent?"

"He was a bit shiny, with a face covered in a grin."

"Well done, now I have a date for you, can you get down to a place near Tunbridge Wells tomorrow about midday, you will need your usual travelling gear, a couple of changes of clothes, you won't be socialising very much but, you will be on a course with one of our new guys who, in fact, will be with you when you travel to Turkey, maybe take a track suit if you have one."

He gave me the address and I asked can I drive it?

"Sure there will be plenty of room to park, and if you are desperate to walk or run each day, there are some ten acres of land, but, you may just want to collapse at the end of the days. Do you have any dietary problems?"

"No, I can tackle anything except tripe and onions."

"Do they still have that expression in the photographic world, it's a good one. I shall be down at the end of the week to see how you are settled in."

"Thanks Douglas, I hope everything goes according to plan with Mr Bent. Like the name. I hope he isn't."

CHAPTER 9

The next day I was up with the larks and on my way. As usual the traffic around Tunbridge Wells was horrendous, but, having weaved my way through, and finding the place at long last, I drove up to a Victorian House that had seen better days. I did notice at the entrance gate, two cameras, pointing inwards so as to not miss anything coming in. It appeared to have a high fenced wall leading off from the gates. So it's protected, I thought. There was a huge semi-circular drive, all with fine stones and several parking places. I took out my large case, didn't want to be short of anything, and rang the bell. It took about half a minute before a stern looking lady, probably in her fifties, opened it for me, I introduced myself. "Yes Mr Sears we are expecting you, did you have a good journey?"

"Well a bit of a problem around Tunbridge, but otherwise usual stuff coming out of London, and the M25 was looking like a big park."

She smiled. "Typical then, I will show you to your room." With that she led off and I followed her up a great sweeping staircase. After she had opened the door she said, "could you come down to the reception desk as soon as you have settled in, it's on your right at the bottom of the stairs, then we can introduce you around."

"Thanks yes, I won't be long." I looked round my room. It had a huge double bed with a deep blue cover, and two small tables, with lights on each side of the bed. A television screen, quite large, and I looked round to see if there was a mini fridge, or anything that was the usual today, but no, it was fairly basic. I looked into the bathroom, there was a bit of rust near the cold tap, but everything else seemed to be in place.

I undid my case and hung out my trousers and suit, put the shirts and rest of my clothes in the drawers and sat down on the bed. Am I jumping the gun, pushing for this training, did I really want to be exposed to danger? which I'm sure will be evident when I get to Turkey, if in fact I am going there. I did have excited feelings and yes, I was anticipating a different part of life now. I am thirty, I've had a few challenges but this seems to be a big one, I would see what evolves whilst I'm here. I had a wash, noticed the towels were huge, and there was a dryer in the bathroom, so I could be content.

I undid my tie, put on a sweater, and went down.

The reception desk was manned by a younger woman who introduced herself as Jane. She was strikingly beautiful, with a full smile and long wavy dark hair. She wanted to know if I had had any difficulty in finding the place, and have I brought my cameras? "We know that is your art."

I replied that I only had a small one which I always carried just in case I witnessed anything of importance. We chatted for a few minutes and she said my compatriot would be with us soon. I gazed around the hall, there were a few scattered paintings, mostly pretty dark and seemed to be country scenes. There was one that stood out, a lighter frame, and it was a photo, yes it was the Queen and she was presenting something to a youngish man who was in a wheelchair. Oh I thought, is this a message, you could be injured in this work. I was about to get closer when a man about thirty five I figured, appeared from the far end of the hallway. He came straight up to me and introduced himself as Patrick. We shook hands and I told him my name. He looked extremely fit and obviously worked out as his handshake was very strong and his shirt, which was open at the neck showed he was in very good condition.

Jane then said. "Welcome you two, I hope you enjoy your stay with us, can you both stand at the bottom of the stairs as Trevor, one of our instructors wants to meet you."

We both shuffled over to where she indicated and looking up we saw a middle aged man waving a piece of paper from the top of the great curving stairs. He loudly said welcome, and with that came rolling down the stairs with his head appearing to be under an arm at high speed, all the way to us, leapt to his feet and pointed a finger at us. We both stepped back a bit and I started to laugh.

He said, "take that seriously. I don't necessarily think you will both have to do that, but for some of our operatives, that would be normal."

It was very impressive, and we both said so, he grinned and said. "It's one of my better moments, welcoming new people. I've never broken anything yet but, I don't know how fit you both are .You look in pretty good shape, but it does help to keep the body supple, whatever you do."

He smiled. "Come with me."

We followed him along the hallway and went into a large room overlooking an impressive garden with a small pond in the middle. There was a blackboard on one wall, several desks and a projector. Um a bit like going back to school I thought.

He said. "Take a seat. You've been told you are on a training course. It's going to be pretty intensive as you only have a few days. It's going to make you very alert to whatever is around you, giving you background on interviewing people, asking the right questions, and, is entirely meant to sharpen your outlook and wits. You will benefit and it will stand you in good stead from a working point of view but, my aim is to sharpen you up. Any questions at this stage?"

We both just stared at him.

"I wondered as I walked here, do you ever use last names?" I asked.

"Whilst we are working we won't use our names much, all you need to know is how we do things and why. Last names are not important here."

"Thanks."

He then said "Let's start at the beginning, Your immediate job is to get to Turkey, to get as near to the border with Syria, best if you can be somewhere near the sea, so as to watch for any groups of people being led, or manipulated towards boats. You will be under the cover of an independent film company, making a film about the problems there, and the future for the refugees."

He looked at Patrick and me then, and said with some meaning. "At all times you must be careful, appear to just be taking pictures in your case Alan, and supporting the filming in yours Patrick. By that I mean your cover is that you are sound, you will be handling the mikes, and adjusting for interviews. When not actually doing this, both of you, if possible, carry on any conversation that you think might be helpful, but most of the refugees will not speak English, so that's one aspect; and not many of them will be open to talk. From the point of view of the people- trafficking, then you must be very careful on any approach, and, in fact you may find it impossible to see or talk to any obvious people that are involved. We think that most of the negotiations take place inside Syria, before the refugees begin their journey's, probably in their towns or villages, but we know that boats are hired, sometimes bought, or owned by the traffickers. So it's going to be difficult to get any real leads. We are initially concentrating on Syria, we know that others from various countries are also trying to get into Europe, but, as far as you two are concerned, it's Syria."

He stopped and had a drink of water.

"The second aspect of this training is observation and concealment, we shall give you plenty of chances to observe, and then report on what you have seen, and, unless you have been introduced to that, you will be surprised at what can be done with a little emphasis on looking, really looking.

Languages, no one expects film people to be conversant in many languages. Are either of you fluent in any foreign one's?" We both shook our heads. "There is a universal language whenever a film unit is around. It's amazing what reactions you will get by just showing up at places, and look to be setting up. Some people will do anything to be interviewed, others will shun it, but those that do help out can easily be sorted as to who is helpful and knowledgeable, or otherwise…

Physical, I suggest we have a run every morning, not too far, but it will help you get your minds fixed on the job in hand, which as you know is going to need one hundred percent concentration.

Feeding while here. You will be well looked after, but, we have a policy of not having alcohol on the premises during a training course. I'm sure you both like a tipple, don't we all, but here it's no, at the end of your course we might well indulge at the local pub - well maybe a half pint." He said with a wide grin.

"Now how familiar are you with the part of the Middle East that we are concerned with. We have a map, so let's see the layout of where you will be. There is indication that the organisation for many of the refugees is becoming planned for the completion of their journey. By that I mean, apparently many now paying, does so through an insurance, and only when they have actually landed in Greece or Italy, will their money be released to the traffickers. This in turn establishes that the traffickers will try to ensure that they get there safely. There is also, again to be certified, that there are shops in Turkey near the sea, that sell tubes, lifejackets, and everything that is associated with journeys by boat, and some of these items may not meet any quality tests. That puts a different view on the whole dreadful operation. It does mean that those financing the operations have some clout with high finance companies. We don't actually know which insurance companies are involved or, if there is more than one company, that is being investigated now."

"Let's look at the map." He took us to a large table on which is a map of the Middle East, pointing out the border between Syria and Turkey. "This is where we believe most of the refugees start their journey. As you can see, it's no great distance from some of the Greek islands, So, your initial target is to get here," pointing at a spot on the map. "We are looking into the best way to get there, flight and then an adapted people carrier, which will be laid on with a driver for as long as it takes. Any questions?"

I had a sneaking suspicion that he knew what we wanted to know. "Are we likely to be under any observation by our own people, by that I mean protected. Should there be any serious people that would like us out of there? And if so, what protection will we have?"

"I did say at the beginning that you were there as an independent film company. You will certainly be protected, but not obviously, in other words, don't spend time looking around to see if there are any people keeping close to you that look like hard SAS men."

That brought a chuckle from Patrick.

I took in that information and then asked. "The obvious thing for us must be getting a feel for movement by refugees. Presumably they will have been told by the traffickers, not to divulge anything that could point the finger at them, as I'm sure there must be plenty of governments eager to find an answer to the problem."

"Yes there is, as you have no doubt seen on the news. There are hundreds, maybe thousands right now trekking across various countries hoping to get to Germany, or any of the countries that will give them shelter, food and drink, even jobs. There will be mothers with kids, it could just be getting cold and remember, they are probably used to reasonably warm winters in southern Syria. But your and our concern is to try to find who is behind the traffickers, you must keep that in mind, however much you are upset by the conditions of the refugees."

I began to really take in why I was being put through this training, also I hadn't as yet had an opportunity to talk to Patrick, He seemed very calm about the situation, I wondered if he had just been put there so as to make me feel it was a joint affair. I think from my initial words with him, that he was Irish, It will be good to talk and find out a bit more of his background.

Trevor now suggested we make a list of our ideas about the programme, how we see our involvement, he said it would help us clarify our own feelings about our venture to Turkey.

I thought that was giving us the chance to analyse our feelings and our reaction to what would be fairly desperate conditions for the refugees.

He said. "Let's take a break. Coffee or tea? I'm going to get lists of our programme for the next few days so you can see just what we will be doing." With that he went out of the door. I wondered if the room was bugged, but asked Patrick what his involvement was, how had he got into M16, He hesitated a bit, then said he had been involved on the periphery for six months now, basically working on a variety of jobs they were doing in the UK and Kenya.

"How did you first get involved?" I asked.

"I was a soldier, saw some of the Irish troubles, then I was working for a film company in Ireland, really as a junior at the end of the troubles. I had been exposed to one or two people that had been blamed for knee capping and, I had been beaten up by three young guys who thought I was spying on them. All I had done was run my camera at them when they were giving two old folk a hard time, They took my camera and smashed it. It was only a cheap one that I was practicing with, as I had a bit of a dream that I could make films. I had seen just about every film that had any real action during the last two or three years.

I managed to get away from them and when I got home my dad was livid and said, "Let's go out and find them, I'll make them wish they'd never been born."

But I managed to calm him down, and it was after that that I met someone in a park when I was taking pictures with my new camera. He asked me if I interviewed anyone after photographing them? Had I ever thought of working for the government as they were always looking for people who were interested in people and research. I also resolved to get fit and to get unarmed combat training, as I had seen some guys and girls in what's today called a boot camp, and they were certainly working hard on it. I've had no exposure to the refugee situation yet and this is to pre-arm me I guess. I can shoot though, I enjoyed the odd times when I could go to a target area and shoot. My dad did too. I think he was more interested than me but it seems I have a good eye."

It was then that Trevor came back into the room. He had a great swathe of papers which he dumped on the table..

"OK you two, its time I gave you a bit of background on what will be expected of you. Firstly I don't expect you to be able to give the sort of welcome I gave you. I do that to keep myself up to scratch for activity if needed. I suggest though, that our running should help with fitness. Its early days for you both, but we want at all times to be up with the news on any activity that we see as possibly dangerous, or harming the state. The state being where we are at any time, and how we deal with problems. Remember the old saying, 'be ready for it when it comes.'

Apart from the physical side, much of our casual information is picked up in everyday life, for instance. In a restaurant, some of our best operatives can listen to multiple conversations and pick up on important points that may casually, or carefully be discussed. Now I wouldn't expect you to be able to do that, as it takes some training and, very keen ears, but, with some practice you can expand your ability. Seeing and registering things. During the training I shall be setting up some displays consisting of a variety of products, and you will be given a short time to acknowledge them, and then test to see how much you have absorbed. As you know you are here for a specific reason, that is, getting into Turkey and finding out as much as you can about the refugee situation.

There are two aspects to this. One to film if possible, the lead up to, and start of a cruise journey for refugees, at the same time try to discover any connections that are related to the financing of the boats, who does that, and the actual setting off from Syria or Turkey.

In your case Alan, you stumbled, we believe, into having a contact that could be very useful from a sourcing point of view. It could be that the person, or persons, that we think are responsible for finance etc., is not him, and we could be totally misled in that, but, in any event you can help through being part of the film unit. You have shown a willingness to be involved with us. We don't expect you to be out of pocket on this adventure, and before we finish our training, I will want an invoice that will cover your time with us. I suggest that we have an initial agreement and if your time overruns, then we will include that on the invoice. Is that ok with you?"

"Yes that's fine, I will work out what I think is fair."

"In your case Patrick, we already have a contract for your involvement but, I think we need to add to that a paragraph on travel and danger insurance, which by the way, Alan, will also be necessary with you."

"Danger Insurance, is that a serious consideration Trevor?"

"Right, let's get down to work," he ignored my question… "Observation. That covers a multitude of sins. General observation in a working environment: always study all aspects of your view say within fifty yards; don't just look at the area you are covering, which you could be familiar with or otherwise. Don't make sudden flips of the head in a new direction, keep a steady vision all around you, watch for sudden movement, watch for anyone staring in your direction, watch for anyone on a telephone looking at you.

Walking or moving from place to place; there are many instances of how people tracking others are described in spy books and thrillers. Make sure that you are not being followed by various means, one good one is to stop and study a window, look at movement across your line of vision, make a mental note of the faces around you, also where possible, the people moving slowly, and ensure you have clocked anyone who has passed you and then stopped, to do what you've done, look in a window. If you know you are definitely being followed, you can always try doubling back on yourself, or if travelling say by tube, take one direction then take another back, and always make sure the first move is away from the direction you eventually want to travel in. A lot of observation is in general activity that you would have if you weren't working in our environment. I'm only highlighting some actions you can take."

With that he opened one of the papers he had brought in. "Look at this."

We both leant over the paper he had spread on the table. It was a photo of a man in a raincoat standing in front of a shop window, apparently looking at some clothes that were on dummies.

"How would you describe that, and where is he actually looking?"

We both studied it for a while, then Patrick said. "He's looking left into the shop window using it as a mirror."

I struggled to see how he could interpret that from the photo, and said so.

"Well", Trevor said, "you are absolutely right Patrick, how did you define that?"

"It's the angle of his head."

I thought this is a bit beyond me. Am I sure I want to be involved with all this cloak and dagger work? I thought when I said I would be interested in being involved with the refugee situation, that I might go on a jolly to somewhere a bit warmer than England, and probably take a few photos, maybe be involved in the odd adventure and come back with a tan. I thought of asking Trevor if all this detailed training, was really necessary for me, but thought better of it and decided I would play along and see where it led, although the danger insurance rankled with me.

We carried on discussing various aspects of watchfulness and then he suggested we have a break.

After some fifteen minutes relaxing and chatting he said "I'm going to lay out a collection of items on the table. Can you both ignore me for a bit and I will call when I'm ready."

We went into a corner of the room which he indicated and sat facing away from him. After a few minutes he called us back and the table was covered in various items, books, telephones, playing cards, there appeared to be about twenty items in all.

"Ok you have one minute to clock all this, then we go over to the corner and you write down what you remember."

I let my gaze slowly wander over the collection, luckily I had a pretty good photographic memory, so I thought I had taken in most of the things. He stopped us and we wandered away, he gave us both a pencil and paper and I started to write, I had reached sixteen different items when he said. "That's it, let's look at your notes."

He scanned mine, then Patricks. "Alan that's good, you have eighty five percent. Patrick not bad, you have about seventy percent of them, but you both missed something that I thought was vital, can you both stay here and think of what you missed."

I wracked my mind and tried to visualise them all again. There was a tiny decorated box, probably just big enough to hold a ring. Had I put that down, I was pretty sure I had, ah!! I've got it, there was a rubber, probably an inch long, maybe more, it had been put alongside a thick box with nail scissors in it. I'd missed that. I wrote it and handed it to Trever, Patrick had his faced screwed up in deep concentration, maybe I had missed more than one item, so I concentrated again. Patrick wrote something down and handed it to Trevor.

He looked at both our contributions and laughed. "Alan yes you've got it. Patrick, you've put two down and you had missed them both, but still no rubber. If I had put a pencil beside it I bet you would both have got it."

I started to wonder what will he dream up next when he said. "Ok let's write what we think will be our best approach to getting information about the traffickers in Turkey."

He gave us both notebooks. I went to the table sat down and thought about it, this was what I had initially reacted to, photography with a filming unit, maybe in Turkey, possibly in Syria. Did I really want all this training in subterfuge, can't I just join the film crew and work on the movement of refugees, am I, really cut out to be a spy, because that seemed to be the route I was now on. I will put these thoughts on paper and see what Trevor's reaction is. Meanwhile I started to write what I thought might be useful in discovering the background to the refugee problem. I had seen some headlines in the papers, but because of my impending trip to Nice I had read more about the situation at Sangatte and the queues for the ferries at Calais. And, the reaction of both the French and UK authorities. On many nights the news programmes would start with some coverage of the refugee situation but, usually when the refugees were either being rescued, or were trekking across miles of land to get to one or other European country. Also, as I was completely out of touch with all aspects of war, and my observations may not be too relevant. I put that I would endeavour to meet and talk to local people in the hotel or where we stayed, meeting locals that spoke English would help, maybe taxi drivers – always up with the news in any country, they might be tapped for information. Other professionals working in the media who were trying to keep up with the situation.

I added a few more observations, mainly concerned with how I thought the setup would be in Turkey. How I might get into conversation with people on the ground there, and was about to hand it over to Trevor, when the thought struck me,

What about Maria and her husband? she had completely slipped from my mind whilst I had been here. Had that short attachment to her been real or imagined. And is my involvement here in any way likely to cause problems for her?

I handed my notes to Trevor, sat down and slipped a look at my watch, we had been working on this for four hours, the time had raced by. Trevor saw me glance at my wrist and said. "Ok fellas, let's have some food, its supper time; you never know, we might have lobster and steak tonight. Let's meet in half an hour by the base of the stairs."

I pointed out to Trevor that I needed to get to my studio to collect some of my photographic equipment.

He responded saying, "Ok, I will come with you tomorrow, say midday, and it would be good for you to make a list of what you need. I may be able to help you with the type of work we will need covered."

I went to my room, I needed a shower, I felt very hot, sticky, and a little tired, it had been some time since I had done this sort of thing. I could happily work in my darkroom for hours if there were certain aspects of developing, the time would be irrelevant and I would continue until I had the desired effect, but observation, tests, studying papers, that went out with my school days.

Having tarted myself up, feeling clean, new clothes on, I was ready for maybe a glass or two and some food when I realised, no drink in this hotel!!! Ah well, maybe the water is good. I wondered why they had the 'dry' setup. But then by the time I had reached the base of the stairs, Patrick was already there. I said, "I wonder if he's going to do the famous roll for our delight." Patrick grinned and said, "I bet he's heard that from wherever he's hiding. Walls have ears" and sure enough Trevor appeared from the dark cavity behind the reception desk and muttered, "so you want me to repeat my performance and then eat."

"You're just trying to impress us, sneaking out from there, but I hand it to you, we should be watchful as you said earlier." I said this with a grin.

"That's it Alan, you never know what is going to happen when you are exposed."

Patrick grunted, "I could eat a horse."

"Maybe you will," said Trevor.

He led us along the hall and we entered a room at the far end, it was quite small with a long table that seemed to take up most of the space. It was set for eight people and Jane suddenly appeared from a door at the rear of the room and said, "water everyone? We've got some smoked salmon as a starter, then a leg of lamb, followed by apple crumble! Good home cooking."

"Great," said Trevor, "that's ok for you guys."

"Sure," we both agreed.

"I won't talk too much shop whilst we eat, but let's deal with our dietary requirements, are either of you suffering from any allergies, or are you on any regular drugs?"

We both answered in the negative.

Our dinner was reminiscent of my school days but enjoyable, after we had finished Trevor suggested we have an early night and meet at seven o'clock for a run. "We will keep it simple, if you've not got running shoes, you should have been told this was possible, that you would run each day. We have several different sizes you can borrow, and a tee shirt, and shorts; maybe run a couple of miles if you're up to it."

I walked off to bed and thought, this is like school days. But I quickly got ready for bed and then wondered if I should keep a dairy of this whole process. Would that be allowed in this situation? I decided I would but not enquire if it exposed me in any way. I had kept the note book that Trevor had given me earlier, that would do until I saw any shops, and that set me thinking. Would I see any shops, would I be shepherded along with Patrick and the film crew all the time, would we get any free time? Suddenly this whole business was taking on a new light.

I wrote the general features of the day, right up to my present thinking, fell into bed and was asleep almost at once. I thought I heard a tapping, rolled over and listened, yes there was gentle tapping at my door, It was pitch black and I looked at my watch which luckily was a little illuminated, eleven fifteen. I slid out of bed went to the door and asked in a very low voice. "Who is it?"

"It's Jane, I need to talk."

I opened the door making certain my left foot was hovering near it as it widened, just in case I needed to stop anyone pushing in. Sure enough it was Jane, she was dressed in a long white dressing gown.

"What do you want, I was asleep?"

"Can I come in?"

"Well yes I guess so, but why?"

"Alan, I'm sorry to wake you, but, I've not really been able to talk to you during the day. There are two things I think you should know; first I saw you looking at the photo of the Queen and the man in the wheelchair. He was my husband; he was on his first mission when he got shot and the result was complete loss of any movement below his waist. He developed into a completely different person to the one I married which, because of his injuries was understandable, but, he eventually left me and now lives with another woman."

"Jane I'm sorry if it's upsetting for you, but where do I come into this story?"

"Alan I think in certain respects you are following the path that he took. He was involved in something that the

86

services got to know of, he was deeply into IT in its early stages, and apparently had ability to break into any circuit, and he was invited to join, exactly as you have been. He was also like you I think, fairly gentle and understanding, he had some deep training here for nearly three weeks, which led him into Ireland doing some undercover work and he was exposed and shot. I met him really during his stay here and we got on well and married. The reason I wanted to talk is to make sure you are aware of the possible danger of going to Turkey, and maybe Syria. I have overheard some conversations that shows we are not at all sure the idea of filming the start point of refugees will be straight forward. I believe we are doing it for many governments, not just the UK. And, Patrick has been with the service for longer than he makes out, he is a trained sniper, what does that say to you?"

I sat down on the bed, Patrick a sniper, that was news and a bit worrying. "Jane I really appreciate your concern. You are correct, I've been led into this set up, but why would they train me by myself, Trevor has not in any way indicated that I would be exposed to danger, although he did mention danger insurance earlier today."

"Perhaps you think I am being indiscreet bringing this to you. Maybe I shouldn't be doing it I suppose, being disloyal to my employers, but, I felt the loss of my husband due to his misfortune and I guess I just didn't want to see another person exposed to danger. Don't report this to anyone, I enjoy my work here, which has its up-side most of the time, if you feel that I am being too careful, forget I spoke to you but, please take care, and make sure you are kept in the picture at all times."

She turned towards the door and was about to open it when I said "Wait a moment, if you overheard conversations, were you meant to? Do you think the powers that be wanted me to be aware of danger?"

She stopped and turned round came right up to me and said, "Alan you are lovely, you are trusting, you are, I believe, a very well respected photographer. I have seen some of the work that you have done, Trevor has been given several copies of your contracts and photographs. Yes they have done much research on you."

I reached out and took her hand "Jane, I noticed you when I came in, you looked calm, beautiful, and warm. I think you have overstepped the line to tell me all this, I respect you for it. I hope it doesn't lead to any trouble, I shall think deeply about what you have told me. I guess it might be a bit difficult to now tell them I want out. Maybe in the light of day I will feel differently, but thanks." I leant forward to kiss her and she responded, we stood close together for a few seconds, she then slipped from my arms, went to the door, blew me a kiss and left, quietly closing it.

Phew! I was certainly aroused in all aspects by my visitor.

CHAPTER 10

The next morning my ringing telephone woke me, it was Trevor. "Up and at 'em Alan, its six forty-five, see you in ten minutes," and he hung up. I felt as if I had been rung out, but swishing my face and teeth then clambered into my trousers and shirt and went down to the reception area.

Trevor was there with some clothes, shoes, and a stop watch, which he flashed at me. "I need shorts and a tee shirt please." He handed them over, running shoes size nine.

Patrick appeared also looking the worse for wear. He was dressed for the run, obviously knew it would happen; I wondered if he had gone through this so called training before. I certainly regarded him in a different light, now I knew he was a sniper. We ran, well we did slow down to a fast walk after about half a mile, as Trever could see I was struggling a little, and we continued at a steady pace until we got back to the house. I went for a shower, we agreed to meet in half an hour for breakfast.

The day was again full on with Trevor leading us through a variety of practices that he said, were useful and necessary. We worked through a sandwich lunch, then he and I went to my studio, driven by a man that appeared in a Volvo as we opened the main door. He didn't say much but took my directions as we neared my studio. Rachel was there and gave me a bit of a dressing down for my lack of contact. She had a list of queries, and after introducing Trevor to her, she and I sat together and went through them. Most of them required phone calls which I said I would make that afternoon, the remaining ones I asked her to write to and explain that I was away on a contract, and would get in touch on my return.

I collected all the equipment I thought I would need, I added my polaroid, just in case I need an instant record. I also gathered some clothes, with some emphasis on middle weight, I always kept a range in the studio, just in case. Put in a pair of swimming shorts, you never know, and some sandals, whilst the season was just about over, I thought it would still be warmish in Turkey. I was about to carry everything out when I realised I would need a passport, got it, and put it into my bag.

Trevor helped load everything into the car, then I went back to Rachel and said. "I'm OK, it's very interesting and I imagine I will be away at least two weeks, I will I trust be allowed to use my phone where I'm going, or I will text you if I need anything. Will you come in most days and keep an eye on the mail and messages."

She nodded looked a bit concerned, but didn't raise any objections, so I said good bye and we left. On the way I told Trevor I had to make a few phone calls and he was fine with that, When I had finished I went back to our briefing room, and we carried on with the training. We broke at six thirty for, 'a wash and brush up,' as he suggested. After another school type dinner, I was ready for bed, and left with Trevor's voice singing in my ear, "see you at seven oclock."

I fancifully wondered if Jane would come to my room again, I had seen her twice during the day, at one bit welcoming three soberly dressed middle aged gents, but had not had a chance to talk to her, which in retrospect was probably the safest thing to do. I'd not made any decision as to whether I would opt out, but as the day went on I realised, I should have made my point already if I really wanted to.

Another day, Trevor said this would be our last one, and he wanted to go through everything we had learnt, just to ensure we were fully aware of our roles in the operation, When he said 'operation,' I had a reaction to the word, that seemed to me to be far more worrying than all that had gone before. But it was too late now to withdraw, and a part of me was actually looking forward to being on the trip. Was it a trip, or was it a dangerous mission? I tried to fathom that out.

Trevor also asked us if we were conversant in any languages. I muttered some French, the odd Spanish word or two, good with Norfolk, (some say a foreign language), but that's all. That brought a chuckle from Patrick, He then said, no Middle East language, and that was all. He seemed a bit more withdrawn today. I still hoped for a real talk with him.

At the end of the day we were introduced by Trevor to an officer, Malcolm, from the Security Services. He explained what we could expect. We were to fly in a military aircraft from Biggin Hill, to a small airfield in Turkey, where we would be met. He repeated many of the points that Trevor had raised, and careful was a word he used many times. We, the UK government, was very concerned about the refugee situation, we have set limits on how many we can accept have been agreed, but, whilst some of our newspapers have made reports about the fragile situations in Turkey and Libya, we will welcome real background to the financing of much initial trafficking, and who is responsible. Malcolm said he was staying overnight and would see us to Biggin Hill, where we would meet the rest of the group.

The next morning we again had a run, this time I felt able

to keep up the gentle running for the two miles, and I made a decision, that when I returned, I would try to keep it up to no doubt benefit. We were introduced to the people we would be with for the next few days, or weeks, there were three of them, and a mixed bunch they were. Dan, the director was very tall, long hair, a wisp of a beard and his face lit up when he smiled. Terry, introduced as the producer, and generally in charge of the expedition. He was very presentable, with a smart suede jacket, brown trousers, and brown shoes, with a white line running around the sealed part. The third was a lady, Jasmine, she was our interpreter and organiser. She was very attractive, long brown hair, brown eyes and a beguiling smile. I felt I would confess to anything if she asked. Patrick had met Dan and Terry previously, but like me he was obviously impressed with Jasmine. We were going to spend some time with them.

Trevor made light of what Patrick and I had done, and that we were pretty well prepared for the journey, and the job. He suggested that I spent as much time in the lead up with Dan and Terry, so as to make sure we were working in harmony.

CHAPTER 11

We all left the next morning and quickly got to Biggin Hill. I felt my usual quickening of the heart, as the thought of flying always affected me. I tried to work out what sort of aircraft it was. It had some twenty seats, very compact, a Red Cross box on one wall, and a small area behind a curtain which appeared to be a small kitchen. It was definitely not a tourist aircraft, basic in its interior, but seemed very fast and quickly climbed to our cruising speed.

The flight was uneventful other than I sat between Dan and Terry, we discussed all aspects of our approach, timing, what to avoid if possible, all the time talking very quietly, Trevor had left his mark. We arrived at a small but obviously often used airfield, there were several Turkish fighters standing around the perimeter. After we disembarked from our flight, we were met by an officer from the British Consulate, who introduced us to a massive man. Amil, who was to be our driver and constant security.

The five of us loaded into his large people carrier, and were quickly driven to a small gateway, waved through after a cursory look at Terry's notes, then suddenly we were out of the airport, no one wanted to see my passport. So this is what being in government hands did.

I was immediately impressed with the traffic handling by the Turkish military that was in evidence around the airport, directing traffic and keeping a watchful eye on everyone it seemed. I wondered if this happened at the main tourist airports, and would it be noticed by holiday makers. Our driver, who spoke pretty good English, talked most of the journey about the situation with the Syrian people running scared in any direction, as long as it was away from the war that raged around them. He said that the traffickers were a very mixed bunch. There were obviously the well organised gangs, charging a fortune to the refugees, and there were some, just opportunists, exploiting the fact they had a rubber boat and would fill it, take the refugees themselves, and return for another load. Loads apparently would appear with frightening regularity. He suggested we may well get the traffickers being very defensive, and in some cases aggressive, so we needed to be very careful in how we filmed them, and how much investigation we had into their background. He said there was a very colourful Frenchman, who he believed, was attached to their consul, appearing at odd times. Amil told us all he had been to the coast a few times delivering various people, journalists, government people, and the like, so he was getting used to the journey and the set up for the refugees. One point he stressed constantly, avoid giving anyone anything, any money or food, if you did, you would be stormed by the masses, as many of them may not have eaten much for some time.

The charity organisations were working twenty four hours a day, but they were overrun with problems and requests. There were several children and families arriving all the time, the refugee camps were overloaded, and it was all a disaster. He made it sound pretty desperate. I wondered if I was up to dealing with these ravaged people. He did have a bright side though and said, we should have decent hotel rooms, whilst there were still a few tourists, it was now near the end of holiday season, so there should be plenty of rooms available, "Wait I minute" I said, "surely our people have booked rooms for us and they would see that were comfortable." Jasmine smiled at me and said, "That was taken care of, we are to stay initially in Kalkan."

"Of course" Amil said, "I was thinking of journalists when I said that." As we progressed we saw a line of refugees walking alongside the road, several women carrying babies or holding hands with young boys and girls. Most of the women were wearing long flowing cloaks, or in the main black dresses. There were not many men in the straggling crowds. Amil said we were approaching Kalkan, and he said, looking at the stream of people. "Many of the refugees have walked or begged lifts on the main motorway from Gaziantep, and they were aiming at Fethiye, some way up the coast. This was reasonably close to giving them a chance to get ferried to Greece. But, we believe there are several starting points, so we will need to work the whole area."

As we approached it looked as if it was a small town, huddled beneath a great rocky mountain. Jasmine directed him to our hotel, set back from the main road. I was very pleased to see there was a garden with a fountain in the centre of a small round pond, in front of the Hotel.

Terry said "Hope there's a swimming pool and its warm."

Jasmine smiled again, "I stayed here fairly recently and yes, there is a pool, and I'm sure you will want to bathe your sore feet after you've spent a day walking around. Remember we are here to work. I know film people like to put their feet up with a glass or two, but I'm sure you might get a few minutes to yourself. All my instructions are to concentrate, and follow up any leads we can get, let's see if we can get enough evidence in two weeks to make it all worthwhile, We, my authorities, have suggested that we should aim at two weeks to get sufficient film and information."

We started to unload our gear, I realised I had brought very few clothes. It had all been hurried when Trevor decided to get us on our way. Amil was helping Dan with his equipment and Jasmine also had a small case, which an old porter lifted out of the car for her and led her into the hotel. We all trooped in, the hotel had a small reception desk and there were a few chairs around the general area. I wondered if it was a tourist hotel, and asked Jasmine if we were near the coast,

"Yes it's quite close a decent walk to it, not much of a place to swim though, quite rocky, but it is a small town that has been very attractive to tourists, and is well served for all things. The best beaches around here are at Patara, if its 'Holiday' and enjoyment, not that you will see it Alan. Tonight I want Amil to drive us along the main road where the refugees are streaming. I don't plan on doing any work although I think you should have your camera with you at all times."

I realised that not only was Jasmine our interpreter but, she had the role of organiser too. I wonder what her real role in the service was? Perhaps I might get a bit of time to sound her out.

My room was comfortable, the décor was of a sandy light brown hue. There was plenty of shelf room for my meagre collection of things I would need, luckily I had brought my international plugs and socket, so would be able to use the electric shaver. That was a plus, so I guess Turkey was pretty up to date with requirements. I went down to the main reception and asked for a bottle of water, I drank deeply and realised it had been some time since I last did that. The others arrived, we all got into the people carrier and Jasmine directed Amil to where she wanted us to be.

As we drove she started to tell us where we should

initially concentrate. "We are well placed here in Kalkan to see and follow refugees as they troop further north to, in their minds, get closer to Greece. Obviously that information has been passed along to them. So we try to find anything that will give us a lead into how they get their information about the traffickers, and, we can work our way up the coast to eventually Fethiye, where we know many of them set off for the Greek islands. I see our role as I hope in their minds, protectors. If we could align ourselves to a group that has a definite meeting place arranged with traffickers, filming on the way, photos, sympathetic discussion, we are here to help, and make a film that could find its way to many of the European countries that would eventually give them home and shelter. I think we want to emphasize that aspect of what we are doing. And eventually meeting their traffickers, that may well give us a lead into who the traffickers are, who finances them, and how reliable all of those involved are."

Quite a speech I thought. I asked Jasmine why she was in our hotel recently. She responded immediately.

"Alan I'm glad you asked that question, I came here with an investigating journalist, a few weeks ago. We came to the same hotel, I was hired as his interpreter, he not knowing, or I believe caring, that I am attached to our government. I had answered his call for an interpreter through some of our contacts, and he had accepted my version of myself. He tried interviewing here, and found, as I have just told you, that most of the refugees were heading further north. He took it upon himself to get us driven to Fethiye. When there he really pushed several people to give him a traffickers story, and in one bar he had led me to, he disappeared for a few minutes. I thought he had gone to the gents, but in effect, he had seen some money changing hands, and had followed someone out of the bar, confronted them, and was shot in the foot. Consequently we had to get him out of Turkey and back to the UK. You Alan, completely out of the blue, managed to get a lead into what we believe is French involvement, and the idea of a film crew, just making a documentary on the situation, was thought up, and here we are. You were eager to help and we did a bit of research on you initially, you may be able to get us the sort of information we need. Not necessarily here, but on return.

Your French connections may be very helpful, and you may also be able to dig deeper into your friend's involvement if any."

"Thanks Jasmine, I'm a bit concerned with the journalist foot shooting though. Did you get any idea of how deep he was in to discovering anything of importance?"

"He played everything close to the chest, nothing appeared in his paper and he refused any medical help here, which we were pleased about. I think that he realised who I was when just the two of us got transported back to the UK, and we landed at Biggin Hill. I had previously travelled with him on BA, which his paper had arranged. But, he wasn't too inquisitive about me particularly as I had got him back, when he thought he might be in danger, if those responsible for the shooting spread the word about him."

I took all that in and then Terry said. "I think in all fairness to Alan we should be open with him. Dan and I have worked together a few times, sometimes dodgy but usually we have worked under a cover name. Patrick, in case you hadn't worked it out, is with us as sound, but, he was a soldier and is our protection, I know we were told that Amil is security, but that is Patrick's role, and he proved himself with Northern Irelands problems. Since then has been co-opted into some of our more outlandish affairs.. Patrick may well be carrying when we start shooting film, and he will judge if he has to really protect us.. Jasmine has proved herself capable of organisation, and can be relied upon to be a saint in disguise."

That brought a couple of whistles from Dan and Patrick, and she flashed them both a smile. "I am really in charge of this whole operation and my aim is to somehow produce evidence of traffickers fleecing refugees, and more importantly, if possible, get a lead on who is responsible. We have some information, but not concrete evidence, and you Alan. Well you apparently staggered into this whole situation by being led up the garden path by what we believe is a French couple, who are certainly shady, and may well be behind much of the financing of traffickers. I hope you don't feel that we have used you, well not in a dangerous way. If there is French involvement perhaps you could be a link that will expose it, and our and several other governments will be very responsive."

I took all this in, yes I was pleased he had opened up to me but, I also felt a bit annoyed that I had to go through the so called training with Patrick. But thinking back, Jane had warned me that night in my bedroom, that I might well be exposed to danger, and that Patrick wasn't just a recruit learning the ropes. However I felt a little let down by their actions. Just what do they expect of me. I covered that with thanking Terry for his openness. We were suddenly surrounded by refugees, some knocking at the windows of the car. I wondered what Amil had made of the talk from Terry. I guess he knew the ropes anyway as he must have heard all the points Terry had made. He was shaking his head and pointing towards the north for the crowd outside the car, and increased his speed a bit to shake them off.

A gap appeared in the people and Jasmine asked him to stop. There was a turning off to the left and she suggested he pull in there. I wondered why, but it was soon evident. Terry, Dan, Patrick, and Amil all got out and were deep in conversation standing at the front of the car, Jasmine and I stayed in as she said "Alan I thought we might have a few minutes together. Is there anything that you want to discuss. Have you been to Turkey before?"

"Well yes, about a year and a half ago, I came with my Australian girlfriend, staying in a four star hotel in Marmaris. We were transported with about ten others from Dalaman, and we had a guide who told us what to expect from the holiday and general stuff about Turkey, but what fascinated me was, on the journey we passed several Mosques, and they all had at least one stork sitting on the top. Our guide said it's a phenomenon here, for some reason they do congregate, maybe it's the call to prayer or something about the roofing on them all, as they don't seem to use other buildings. When we did arrive at Marmaris we were not too impressed with the hotel, and on the second day we took a boat trip and found a lovely little village, called Turunc. We both fell in love with it, found a self-catering aparthotel and decided to stay there. We found all the Turks most friendly and accommodating, we spent some days on the beach, others on a superb yacht, it seemed that the best way to travel around that area is by boat. In fact on the last day of our two weeks we went back to the hotel in Marmaris by boat.. That's all I recall about Turkey."

"Ok so basically all this is new to you, as is no doubt our set up. We are working with other governments on the whole problem of refugees, because we believe that there will be some who are not just getting out of Syria, but are trained Isis people. Turkey has placed quite a number of their security people in the straggling groups, usually making their way to one of the Greek islands. These people are recognised by certain attitudes, and at the moment Terry is watching the crowds to see if he can spot any. He has been in touch with the Turkish security services discussing our activities, and that we are now ready to start our programme."

I noticed virtually as she said it that Terry walked over the road and linked arms with a tall man that was walking with the crowd. They appeared to be in conversation for some minutes until he released his arm and came back to the car. As he and the others climbed in, there was a roar as a helicopter swept overhead at a very low level, hanging from the side was a cameraman, filming all the refugees and us. Some of the refugees flung themselves to the ground, no doubt a reaction they had discovered during the attacks in their home towns.

Terry snapped at Amil, "Turn round, let's get back to the hotel."

I wondered what had caused the hurry, it all seemed very slow moving and the crowds were, I thought, pretty much under control, just walking towards a nasty voyage, their death, or a new life.

As we started back Terry's phone beeped, he listened his face going grey, "No I can't believe it, the bastards, are you OK? I will call when we get back to our hotel, I want all the background." With that he shut down his phone and as he was sitting in the front seat he turned and said. "Isis has attacked Paris, They've co-ordinated some attacks, there is a running fight going on at present. Several dead. They think the ringleader has got away."

"Is Doug OK Terry"? Jasmine asked.

"Yes, he's now in the middle of organising some of our people to get involved."

"Well that gives us all the more reason to weed out any of them in this mob if we can," she pointed to a thinning crowd of refugees.

I sat very still trying to get my mind round what Terry has just said, Paris attacked, it was only last year that the publishing company, Charlie Hebdo was devastated. There must be some high level planners in France, I guess they will take some weeding out, am I in a war, how have I got to this situation? It was only a week or so ago, I was contentedly snapping cars in Nice. We were all affected by the news, and we were very quiet with our own thoughts as we pulled into the hotel drive.

During our meal that evening Terry said he had further information about the attack, and the main group came from Belgium. To make matters worse, the police had interviewed the brains behind the attack and let him go into Belgium, so there were some red faces in France, and a huge manhunt was being operated. It shouldn't affect our operation Terry finished by saying. "Tomorrow we try to get alongside a group that has a definite arrangement to meet traffickers, then we must make it seem that we are doing a documentary on them all the way, until they actually board their ferry. We discussed various options, and eventually went to bed, all of us in sombre mood.

CHAPTER 12

I slept well and woke at 6.35. I decided I would go for a short run. Luckily I had packed some shorts and a tee shirt, plus I had my old pair of sailing shoes as I called them, a bit tattered, blue with a thick sole. I set off from the hotel and turned left out of the drive. We had passed through the small town on the right yesterday when we arrived and I thought I would see what happened in the other direction. I was quite surprised to notice that it was very quiet, particularly after the constant noise last night of the refugees and traffic. I was impressed, there were a few birds singing, and as I passed out of the town there were some detached houses, with quite big drives, then further along I saw a flock of sheep and, in the next field were some goats. This is so peaceful I thought, and no refugees? I ran a little further and turned a corner to see a woman with two small children sitting on a bench. It was well set back under some overhanging branches of a tree. She was comforting one of the children it seemed, and she waved and beckoned to me. I looked around, there was no one else in either direction, so it was obviously me she was signalling. I stopped running and walked up to her feeling wary, I was ashamed of that feeling but, I suppose having so much indoctrinated in me about the reaction of refugees and jihadists, I was right to be careful. I wondered if she spoke any English, she appeared to be about thirty odd, and the children looked probably seven and five.

I was surprised as I drew near she said in perfect English. "Can you help, none of us have eaten, or had anything to drink for nearly twenty four hours, we have rested and tried to sleep on this bench, but we all need water, please do you have any?"

I thought of all the water we had had the night before at the Hotel, we had consumed very little alcohol, "I'm sorry, I have none with me and my hotel is a little way away."

"Would it be possible to get some for us?"

"Yes, please wait here. I will see what I can get. Why are you alone, there are no other refugees around, did you just stop here? as there were several all walking in that direction yesterday." I pointed back the way I had come.

"My husband has gone ahead to try to find a way of getting to Greece, he will arrange a crossing and we will carry on today until we find him, but, we really need to refresh ourselves and the children are desperately tired and hungry."

"Was there no charity food on the way?" I asked.

"Not since yesterday morning, and we walked all day until we found this bench."

"I will get some water for you, and see if I can also buy some food."

I then set off at pace but the thought suddenly hit me, I had not arranged for any money, it had not crossed my mind. I probably had a few euros from my Nice trip, I'm sure the hotel will let me use my credit card, because I was now determined to get some provisions for the family, and I would like to talk to the lady. I will also take my camera, as this is definitely a chance to get some background.

I looked at my wristwatch, it was now seven fifteen, Jasmine had asked us to meet at seven thirty.

I quickly got back to the hotel, Terry was standing outside the main entrance, I was surprised to see him with a cigarette in his left hand.

"Hi Alan," he greeted me," you keeping in shape?"

"Terry I have an opportunity." I explained what had happened and pressed him on being able to spend on my, or our behalf, for the hotel to provide some food and water for the family.

"Sure," he said, "let's go into the kitchen, I will do that whilst you get your camera."

"Shall I try to get her involved with us?"

"I think if you try to get her intimidated into reasons we are here, she might clam up."

"Ok, I'll get the camera."

I got back down in a few minutes, went to reception and asked the man there if he had seen Terry? "Yes he is in the kitchen," at that moment Terry came out with a plastic bag looking fairly full.

"Look, I've got some hard boiled eggs, which they were going to use for salads at lunch, several slices of bread, a little cheese, four apples and some water."

"That's great Terry, I will deliver."

"I've thought about your approach. Ask if it's possible to catch up with her and her husband later and follow their progress. You could say that you do some work for magazines and newspapers in the UK and they are always interested in the refugee situation; also ask where she's from, what her husband does, and have they any particular country they are aiming for?"

"Terry, I would have done that anyway, I'll see how much I can get from her without pushing too hard but, I bet that as I've provided this for her, she might be willing to talk a bit." With that I set off, so I would have my exercise anyway today, and it might be fruitful.

When I got back to the bench, one of the children was lying with his head on her lap, and was obviously asleep. There was still no sign of any other refugees, and only one car, and two lorries had passed me on the way to her.

I opened the bag and told her what was in it, she heaved a great sigh of relief and thanked me. She managed a smile and woke up the little boy, speaking in her own language.

I tentatively asked her how long she had been walking, and what risks did she feel they, as a family were taking?

She gave each of the boys a piece of bread, an egg, and some cheese, she gave them each a small bottle of water, she also drank deeply from her own, had a bite of her bread, and a piece of cheese.

She then looked at me with tears in her eyes and a great soulful smile of thanks. I felt moved by the experience.

She then said. "There is no alternative, but to try to escape the horrors of the war in Syria, we know the dangers that we face but, we would rather drown seeking safety and freedom, than stay in Syria, where for the last several months we have spent so much time in shelters and bunkers, avoiding battles raging around us. Our street was hit three times by bombs and the last one blew out our windows, so three weeks ago we collected all we thought we could carry, rescued all the money we could and left, knowing we faced more danger. But, two days ago, we managed to cross the border, we had been given a lift with five others, all wedged tightly in a lorry full of smelly fruit by a sympathetic Syrian, and made it here last night, well near, fairly near, and we have walked to here since then."

"I admire your courage, and your ability to speak English, have you ever been?"

"No, but in university it was my speciality, I wanted to

learn it and wanted to be a teacher, but I got side-tracked and ended up as a translator for conferences and business companies."

"What about your husband what does he do?"

"He is a doctor specialising in skin grafts, and until a year ago had a shared partnership with two others in private medicine. He was attached to a hospital until a bomb wiped out almost three quarters of it. He saw the desperation of all the patients that were still alive, the hospital was closed down and virtually disappeared as the war reached its present heights, or lows. He has been like a general practitioner since then, until we saw that the situation couldn't possibly improve unless there was some sort of settlement, and we decided we would leave."

"Where did you live?"

"Aleppo."

"Oh Aleppo. Yes we have seen news of the trials of your town. Does your husband speak English too?"

"He has a fair ability, that's probably because I have insisted that we speak it often in our family, so both my sons are used to it, and are both passable."

"Have you any idea which country you actually want to get too?"

"We think with our qualifications we would be welcome in Germany, probably Italy, and the UK. At this moment in time we are out of Syria and we don't have to spend hours sheltering from gunfire and bombs. What is your name so I can thank you properly?"

Oh, I was suddenly made to consider myself, I was so keen to hear her news that I had not for a moment considered any sort of introduction. "My name is Alan. I am a freelance photographer here to see if I can help in any way to let the world know what it's like to be a frightened refugee, seeking to find a home."

"Alan, I thank you from the bottom of my heart for your kindness and interest. My name is Yasmin, If we should ever make it to England, we would like to thank you in the very best way that your country would recognise."

"Well that's kind, but I am with a film crew who are trying to make a documentary of this whole incredible situation, and now hearing this from you, I wondered if we could travel with you, help out wherever we could, and record your trials and tribulations. To use an old English saying."

"I'm sure you could, and I'm sure my husband would also be agreeable. We intend to set off soon and we are to follow this main road until we catch up with my husband."

"What if we were to help transport you some of the way?"

She looked a little suspiciously at me when I said that, and I wondered if I had been too keen to get that across.

"What would that entail if I said yes?"

"It would not bind you to anything other than it would firstly help you and your children, and secondly it would help us create the documentary which we are preparing."

"But what would I or we, when we get to my husband, be expected to do?"

"We would make a filmed documentary, looking at the perils involved in the long walk to get to a place where it would be possible to arrange a ferry crossing to one of the Greek Islands. Film you actually leaving and probably ask you or your husband, a few question regarding what prompted you to leave Syria, some reference to how dangerous it was in your home. Your recollections of the journey and your hopes for the future. In return for that we would be pleased to transport you at least to your husband, perhaps it might be useful if you talked to our producer of the documentary. He would certainly be able to fill in any details of our programme. I am hired to photograph the situation here and cover the refugees departure from Turkey. I can arrange for him to meet you now if you want too. It's not far to walk to our hotel."

She looked at her children, they were both silent, they both looked very tired, and, the younger one appeared to be ready to sleep again given the chance. She pondered what I had said then nodded and said. "Thank you Alan, we are in a bad place, but I can't see how we would be of much use to you other than your film crew just following us on our route . I would be prepared to talk about our problems in Syria. How we see the future there, explain our predicament, and generally outline our hope for work and care for our children."

"Let's go to the hotel and you can discus everything with our producer. Is your young one up to walking? he looks a bit fatigued."

"I'm sure he is," and with that we set off. I hoped Terry was around and available. I didn't know how the hotel will react to my bringing refugees to it.

When we arrived I asked her to wait near the entrance and bumped into Terry, who was just leaving the dining room, "Early breakfast," I asked,

"Yes much to do, will see you in a bit."

"Wait Terry, I have brought my refugees, and I think she will co-operate with us. I suggested to her that as you were the producer of this documentary, it would be more helpful to talk to you. She's ready to work with us, she has her two sons with her. She speaks perfect English, she worked as an interpreter and, her husband's a doctor. He has gone ahead to try to find a way to get to Greece, she has to stay on the main road here until she catches up with him. I have suggested we might be ready to give her transport until we find him."

Terry looked a bit dubious, but then said. "Let's try it,

what's her name?"

"Can you believe? Yasmin."

He gave a sly smile. "That could be meant."

We walked out to the door, she was standing just outside peering out to the road,. Terry walked to her and extending his hand said, "Welcome. Alan has been talking to you I understand and you, like everyone else, are trying to get to Greece."

"Yes we are, but we are depleted, my husband has gone ahead to see if he can negotiate a ferry or boat crossing to get us to one of the islands."

Terry smiled at her and said, "I understand you have slept on a bench further along, luckily Alan here is a bit of a fitness fanatic and he came across you when on one of his runs. I believe he has given you some food too. He has told you what we are doing, that is, making a documentary on the situation for people like you. We want to show what resilience you all have, how difficult it has been to get this far, and then, we want to show how you are all setting off for the Greek islands. It will be sympathetic to your cause, and we hope will help to enable you all to settle in different countries. I understand you are an interpreter, do you speak other languages in addition to English?"

"Yes, I am reasonably fluent in German, and Spanish, very limited in Italian, and I was until three months ago, starting with Russian, as we thought the time would come when the Russians would back Assad, and we believe they are helping now with bombing the anti-Assad groups."

Terry was obviously impressed with her responses and said. "Please come in, find a chair, would you like tea or coffee, and would your boys like some juice?"

"I would welcome a sweet tea, I think I need some revival, I'm sure the boys would like orange or coke if you have any."

Terry went back into the dining room and I sat down with her. She was exhausted but managed to keep a distant smile on her face as she told her boys I guess, in her own language, that they were getting drinks.

I said. "When Terry comes back I will leave you with him, as I need to change from this running gear and have a little breakfast myself."

"Oh I'm sorry, I didn't mean to keep you from eating, when did you arrive here in Turkey?"

"Yesterday. Seems like a long time ago now."

Terry came back with a tray, on it were some croissants, tea, and fruit juices, I excused myself and went up to my room, I felt very animated, it seemed that I had had a stroke of good fortune running into Yasmin, she could be the very lead we're looking for. I quickly changed into my regular clothes washed, and went down to the dining room. Terry was deep in conversation with the proprietor of the hotel. I wandered into the dining room. The others were there crowded round a small table, they shuffled up a bit, and I was able to join them.

Jasmine enquired had I slept well, Patrick gave me a big wink and said. "Not up for a run this morning?"

"I've done that and now I thought a bit of Turkish nosh with some smoked salmon and scrambled egg would be good for me."

"Some chance of that," said Patrick, "better enjoy some muesli and nuts, good for your brain."

"Brain's not too sharp at the moment," I said, "but am working on it, have had some success though." Then I told them what had happened, and that Terry was dealing with another Yasmin at the front of the hotel.

"That's great, what shape are they in?" Jasmine asked.

"Pretty tired. They slept on a bench, well they tried to, but, they all looked washed out. The surprising thing is that there were no refugees at all when I was out there about an hour ago initially, just the three of them. She said they had been given a lift in a lorry with a few other refugees, mainly men, to a town, she thought was named Kas which I think is about ten miles towards Syria." Her husband and the others that were in the lorry had gone on, but her children couldn't walk any further. They had found this bench, quite well protected from the road, but then it's very quiet today, I only saw one car and a couple of lorries in probably half an hour."

Jasmine then said. "Well if Terry can persuade them to be part of our so called documentary, we might as well get on with it. So let's get all the equipment necessary and move off, maybe it might be an idea to leave this hotel and move anyway up nearer the embarkation area."

"Are you suggesting that or ordering it?" I enquired, "because I will pack my luxury bag now and happily leave."

The others all nodded. I noticed that Amil was particularly quiet today. Maybe he's feeling the pressure, or maybe he's not paid to voice too many theories.

Having quickly eaten, we trooped out to the reception, Terry and the three were sitting on the chairs that were there. Yasmin stood up when we came in, she looked a little lost with all the movement. Our Jasmine held out her hand and warmly shook Yasmin's, "I hope you are settled and have had something to eat and drink."

"Yes we have, and we are planning to come with you to, I hope, find my husband and his friends."

"Do you need to have a wash or freshen up?" asked Jasmine. Ah, ladies I thought. Always think of the necessities in life.

"Please, and can my two sons have a wash too? my husband is carrying most of our things, we thought necessary, so a wash would be welcome."

Jasmine led them off to the washrooms and Terry said.

"I've discussed our programme with her, she is more or less in agreement that she will co-operate, but, only if she is not exposed to any danger, to her and her family, more than she has already experienced. I assured her that we were supported by the Turkish authorities to make this documentary, and we would be protected should anything dangerous come up. As far as she was concerned, we were making a newsworthy film which could only be of help to all refugees, whatever country they came from."

Dan then asked. "How do we keep them in our care, by that I mean, ensuring they don't wander off or get snapped up by traffickers?"

"It means we have to be very watchful at all times, and when the actual handing over of money takes place, that could be difficult, and probably dangerous."

"Then we need to plan that now really, and try to ensure she understands what her, or her husband's role will be. I would assume he will want to do any negotiating when they get to the traffickers."

"Yes I'm with you Dan, in fact I think the travelling and general filming shouldn't be too demanding, but, the end result is what we are after so. I presume we travel with her, then, if and when we get to her husband, I guess we will have to accommodate them. Jasmine can look after that."

"Did you mention that Terry, that we will arrange accommodation for them?"

"I did say, we hope they will keep with us and as yet we have not decided where we will stay, when we do, they can have a family room with us, she took that in and thanked me."

CHAPTER 13

Luckily our people carrier had three rows of seats so we were all able to have reasonable comfort and we set off. After a few miles, we caught up with a ragged stream of refugees, walking, pushing prams, one pulling a basic cart full of objects. Yasmin asked Amil to drive slowly, so she could look for her husband. I asked her." What time last night did he leave you and the boys?"

"That was about nineteen thirty so he should be well on his way, but I will keep a watch, one of the refugees with us in the lorry was very tall, so if they are together, he will be easy to spot."

"I was amused that she said nineteen thirty, It would have been seven thirty to us I'm sure. Ah the continent!!

We cruised slowly alongside the people, some were hardly able to walk, being very old, some carrying babies and small children, some obviously just very fatigued. We passed a charity feeding point, there were many sitting in the road, on the banks, on rocks that were on the sea side of the road, some even sleeping, stretched out wherever they had collapsed. I guess the shattered travellers were trying to get a few fitful hours of sleep, even though they were on uncomfortable hard ground.

Yasmin said "I can't see him in that crowd."

I said, "why don't you get out of the car and stand looking at them all, then if he is there he would no doubt see you."

"Is that alright?" she asked Terry.

"Yes, fine, I suggest you just wander a little along the line, we will drive beside you." After some shifting around in the car she was able to get out and walk, very slowly along the gathering. After some one hundred yards she came to the end of the resting party, and with a last look around, she climbed into the car.

We set off again, Amil driving very slowly, as we approached Gelemis. We again caught up with several refugees, many keeping close and on a pavement now. There were a few well spread out houses on the coast side of the road, but inland, it was getting very rocky and mountainous. Yasmin again studied all the people as they walked, without it seemed any recognition. We came to another charity group providing water and clothes. There were a few refugees sitting around the table where the drinks were, but no husband. I could see she was getting frustrated, and now the boys were beginning to get irritated with the proximity of us all, and they obviously wanted to let off steam.

Terry suggested we stay for a short while and all have a walk around. "We could film the charity people and maybe make contact to see if there was any relevant news." Dan and Patrick unloaded the film equipment, I selected my camera and we went over to the table. There were two ladies and one man on the table Terry introduced himself, and one of the ladies answered in English.

Terry said. "We are making a documentary on the refugees and creating a story about the situation. How long have you been providing help?"

She said. "We try to get here most days, we have a few

church people, and a mosque that are collecting the clothes you see, and money for water. Some days, we can offer pittas, and the odd cake. The refugees seem to be very controlled and not at all demanding, just grateful for someone to care about them. But then we have heard some frightening stories, particularly from the Syrians."

Terry said. "Yes we have, in fact we have a Syrian lady with us with her two boys, her husband has gone on ahead to try to arrange a ferry, or some form of transport, to get them to Greece, do you know where most of the boats are setting off from?"

"There are several places I believe, we've not actually been involved with that part of their travels, and, according to one or two people in the town, it can be quite difficult and dangerous to get involved with some of the organisers of boats. They insist on money up front, and once the boat has left they disclaim any interest, but, as you probably know, there have been many deaths. Also it seems that some Turkish shops are selling life jackets that are dangerous, because they are padded with a material that actually gets heavier when wet."

"That must be stamped out, can't the authorities intervene and close the shops."

"It's very difficult as we believe they are spread along the coast, how can you possibly advise thousands of refugees of the danger? They may well find some mounted boards on their route telling of the dangers but, they are so determined to get away, that they may well just ignore things like that."

"Do you mind if we film you at the table handing out the water and clothes?"

"Of course you can, our gentleman here speaks Syrian, and a bit of English if you want to catch any words."

Terry brought up Dan and Patrick, they set up the camera and Terry held a microphone, I wondered if it was live or just a show.

A few of the refugees started to take an interest in the set up, and moved in a bit to be nearer the table, Terry asked the lady "Are you here every day?"

"No I'm not, I usually work here three days a week, and have been doing so for several weeks. There are ten of us taking turns to spend time at the table. We have several young men that collect the clothes, and we have one wonderful lady that bakes cakes every week. and they get distributed on certain days. The refugees are mostly very grateful for our help, and most of them thank us, sometimes in Turkish, sometimes in their own language. John here speaks Syrian, so he will interpret, and we get some flowing speeches, saying how much it means to them, as many will have walked many miles, sometimes over three or four weeks, with very little proper rest, and not much food. As the season for growth is just about over, there are not many crops, or apples, or fruit, on the side of the roads, so we, and other charity tables are their sole providers. But, they always seem to be restrained in receiving the food and water we provide."

"Thank you, what is your name and where did you learn your English, it is very good."

"My name is Marcia, I was born near Birmingham. My mother is Turkish, my father an engineer in the Oil industry, and he found his way here many years ago. We enjoy life here in Turkey, where you will find the very best figs in the world." She said this with a broad smile.

Terry laughs at that. and asks John.

"I suppose most of them speak their own language, is English used a lot in Syria?"

"Very few speak English well, and most of them hardly know any words at all. What you have to realise is that these refugees are a total mix of what you would call a class in

118

England. Their one concern is getting away from terror, and speaking a foreign language is probably their last concern."

"Thank you John, we will see if we can talk to one or two of the refugees, have any of these near the table actually talked to you?"

John looks around," I can't point any out to you, if you wait alongside the table here as they come up for their clothes or water. I will point out those that do."

"Thanks," with that Terry retreats a few yards and Dan then scans the refugees with his camera until he has covered most of those waiting.

Some of them seeing the camera is closed down now come up to the table and collect their water. It seems that is the priority for them, John greets them all warmly, asking if they need clothes and at the sixth man that answers, he nods to Terry, and asks the man if he will talk to him. The man hastily backs away, then turns and hurries over to a little group . John just raises an eyebrow and continues to talk to those that are coming up. The same happens again with another man, and it was the third one that John nods at that seems prepared to talk. Terry asks Dan to hand hold the camera and record the interview.

Terry shakes the man's hand, The man is wearing quite ragged clothes, trousers that are holed at the knee and a sweater that is tangled, and part of the base of the wool is hanging down.

"Have you come far?" Terry asks.

The man nods.

"Do you mean you have been walking for many days?"

"Yes, many days. I have some children."

"How many?" asks Terry.

"Four, one is a girl, she is very sick."

"Have you reported that to the charity people here. and at the other places?"

"Yes but no doctors."

"What sort of sick?"

"She is sick every day."

"Physically sick, how old is she?"

"Ten and four, she is fourteen."

Terry looks puzzled, "Perhaps you can get her examined here in this town. Can we help to find a hospital?"

"Yes please, she is very sick."

Terry turns to John who is having a heated discussion with Marcia about the need for more water.

"John would there be any chance of getting this man's daughter to a hospital for a check? she is very sick every day."

"Perhaps, but it will be a long wait at any time of day, can he tell you how long she has been like this?"

Terry asks the man and he says. "Since we arrived in Turkey, it took us many days to get over the border, and since then she has been sick."

Dan had been standing quietly alongside Terry filming this and he whispers, "Could she be pregnant?"

Terry says "I wondered the same thing, but how would I possibly ask her father? being no doubt ruled by his religion."

Terry again turns to John, "If I offered a lift to the man and his daughter could you direct me to the hospital, then perhaps he can stay with her until she is assessed, then he would have to find his way back here again."

"You could. The hospital is probably half a mile away. It might be better if the mother went with her, but on second thoughts, if they all went, then the rest of the family could wait at the hospital, probably be given some food there, and then all being well, could carry on their walk to the north. I doubt if any of them will speak much Turkish, so it could be very difficult to sort it all out. Maybe Ali, our third lady will lead them to the hospital, let me ask her."

He went to the far end of the table and asked her and she initially shook her head, but then he persevered as she seemed to reluctantly agree.

He came over to Terry and said, "Ali has agreed to take them and point out how they can get back to this road so they can continue, did you get anything useful in your talk with him?"

"Not really, other than the fact that this whole affair is completely savage, how can these people ever find any resolution to their problems, as no doubt the same is happening to many of them. You have to admire their courage, but, I suppose if you have lived through a war going on around you, this is peace comparatively."

Terry was obviously upset at the incident, but he then said to the man. "This lady is going to take you all to the hospital where you can wait, and perhaps your wife can go into the hospital with your daughter, and you may be able to get some food while you wait."

"Thanks you. Thanks you," said the man, and he hurried off with Ali.

"Thanks John," says Terry. "I don't think I will press the point with any others at the moment."

Dan finishes filming and said, "How can they survive, not speaking the language, not presumably having any money, food or clothes. That will be a headline when we get back."

"I don't think we are looking for headlines Dan, but I agree, I really feel for that man and his family. I never got the chance to ask him about Syria, what he did, or how they got out of the country. I just got involved with his predicament, and that became important to me."

I had been standing with Jasmine alongside the car. Amil was talking with a small group of refugees, and Yasmin and her children were fast asleep in the car. We were both watching Terry and Dan, we were out of earshot, but it was evident that both of them had been affected by the man. I asked Jasmine if she had had any opportunities to get real information from any refugees on her last visit with the journalist, and she said.

"No, not really, we were constantly on the move, and he was very insistent on doing any interviews by himself, unless he needed an interpreter. None of the conversations I was involved with were very fruitful in information terms, but, I did notice that around the charity tables there seemed to be much more rubbish, just jettisoned by the refugees. That seems to be tidied up. In fact, look around, apart from a few sleeping on the sidewalk, everyone else were sitting on the ground eating or drinking what those at the table have given them. Also there were several policemen on my last visit. I've yet to see one on this. I know we've only been here a day, but there are none around, I wonder why that is?"

I couldn't add anything to that, so I said. "I'm very impressed by the attitude of the refugees, they all seem to be so careful not to upset or distract anyone from helping them, or at least supporting them. I suppose most of the Turks we meet here are just thankful that they don't appear to want to stay in Turkey, just use it a hopping off place."

"Well yes, but so far we have only been exposed to this main road when we arrived yesterday, it has been our route since we left this morning. I'm sure we will see a very different way of life when we get close to the stepping off places. There doesn't seem to be any places just along here that are being used as starting points for ferries."

I changed the subject. "Jasmine, it looks like our family is catching up with some sleep. Can we leave them for a while, do you think? I guess they walked for maybe twelve or thirteen hours yesterday, quite a slog I imagine, and those little kids. No doubt they would take some holding back from make believe. I wonder if the father left them earlier, and hurried to get further along."

"Alan, he must have spent some time discussing that with his wife, I suppose the chances of her not finding him might be possible, but, I guess they will have had some idea of the sort of reception they will get when they meet the traffickers, stuff like that will be passed on. He probably felt held up by the kids and wanted to get their lives sorted out, so she can just join in when they are all together at their starting point."

I nodded and said, "I see that Patrick was watching over Terry and Dan while they were filming, he's a quiet bloke, and I never got to talk at all seriously with him when we were on our training gig."

"You're right, but I'm glad to have him on our side, he was very well referred to in Northern Ireland and made his mark there."

"Shall we join Amil?" I said. "We might learn something."

"Yes OK."

We carefully avoided three youngish girls, all stretched out on the sidewalk. Ah that's interesting I thought, a sidewalk, that must have been very forward looking by the local council. We were on the edge of the town, but I wondered how many local people would have used it before the influx of refugees, and there were very few cars or lorries passing through, so it wasn't a hub of activity.

When we got up to Amil, he gave us a great grin and said he was enjoying talking to this family who have been travelling for five weeks to get here. They have walked, been given a ride on a horse and cart, in a lorry with live sheep, and to top it all, in an open car in Syria with a singer, not a top star, but he sang to them for about fifteen miles as he drove. That was their highlight. They had also gone three days without any real food, just corn and vegetables that were growing in fields where they were walking. They are headed for Fethiye further north, they heard from friends that had a telephone that, there were several organisations set up to arrange ferries to Greek islands.

Jasmine thanked him and asked the man in the group if he had names and addresses of these organisers of ferries?

"Yes he did," and he fumbled in his back pack and gave her a sheet of paper which she studied. Then wrote down several things and handed it back. She smiled at him and uttered something which sounded like, I love you, well to my untrained ear it did, but I will ask her when we finish with them.

Amil started to talk to them again and they had an animated talk with much arm waving and pumping of hands.

Jasmine also shook hands with the man and the three women, one looked very pale and was trembling a bit. We wandered back towards the car. "What did you say to the man? It sounded like, I love you to me."

She laughed and said, "Alan, I think your imagination knows no bounds, as we like to say in Stratford."

"Are you from Stratford?" I asked.

"Yes I was brought up there and should have been an actor, but I couldn't remember my lines."

"Oh yes, and then what happened?"

She laughed again, "Alan, I loved the swans on the river, I was jealous of the queen, as they were hers, or so my dad said. But, I never got too interested in acting. I did enjoy much of what Shakespeare wrote, and took some time over some of the plays. I particularly like, A Midsummer Night's Dream."

"Phew. Must be good. I'm from Norfolk, in case you didn't read that about me, and my roots are pretty deep there. In fact, I can sing some of the Norfolk Postman's Songs, which no doubt you will ask me to do when we finish this job. Any likelihood of any social when we get back?"

She looked hard at me and I fidgeted a bit. Not a word passed her lips, I gave her a minute and then said. "Well we might get to know each other a bit more by the end."

"Alan, I am very settled in my job, I love the theatre, I enjoy sailing, I tried to play a bit of golf, bit of snooker, I like playing cards, poker maybe, can recite yards of poetry, I love food and wine. There you have me, summed up in less than a minute. What would we talk about?"

"Phew, that's great. I believe there's a competition when competitors can rattle off dozens of facts and relevant things, and the winner is given a medal, and it's called, super speed. No doubt you've won it countless times?"

"No, but I might just enter it now you've enlightened me."

"Jasmine, it's wonderful to work in a totally different environment. Whilst I was somewhat overcome with it all when doing my so called training, I now feel I could be of help in the 'undercover world,' and would enjoy it."

"Alan, don't get carried away, it's been plain sailing so far, but, I have no doubt things will get much more difficult, and we may well be stressed out by the time we have gathered all we want."

"So that's a maybe is it? I'm sure you're right, we've had no aggravation at all so far, everyone has been easy to get on with. The refugees are, or at least appear to be, very normal people, trying for a new life. Maybe tomorrow or the next day, we may get to the difficult scene in this play, when we start seeing the hard bit of their journey."

"I don't doubt that for a minute, no doubt you have kept up to date with the newspapers, there are horrific things going on, I'm sure we will see some here before we leave."

With that she went over to Terry and Dan. I thought

about what she had said, she didn't mention if there was a fella involved in all her activities, I studied her at a distance. She was certainly attractive, probably five foot five in height, very well proportioned, if a little muscular. With light brown hair that was brushed straight down on either side of her head. Great lips, hey steady on boy, I know you've not been let loose on anyone for a while, but I think it would be pretty difficult to get to the real Jasmine under the work ethic. I wandered over to them. Terry had not asked me to take any photos of the people he had been interviewing, I wondered about that, why the filming if not stills? Must be a reason.

"Hi Terry was that informative?"

"Yep Alan, in its own way. Dan thinks it's highly relevant to what's going on and will certainly feature in anything we produce."

"Do you want me to do anything here? Yasmin and her two kids are flat out in the car, catching up on their sleep. Amil has an interesting family, they've been travelling for five weeks, and had a variety of transport. They were even picked up by a pop singer who sang to them. I wondered if anyone had what we would call, a normal life in Syria but obviously they do."

As if a signal had been given several of the refugees got up, collected their things, and fell into groups and started walking northwards. Some fathers were carrying kids on their shoulders, there was one or two prams, little groups of people helping the elderly to walk, and within ten minutes the area was virtually clear.

The three people manning the table started to tidy things and arrange the clothes they had left in some sort of order, there were several sweaters and a few trousers for men. Heaps of coloured clothing for women, and a collection of shoes under the table. As a keen shoe collector, I had a look, some seemed to be new, there were several sandals, and just one or two high heeled ladies shoes.

I grinned at Jasmine and said, "how is your shoe situation? There are some good walking shoes here, particularly the high heeled ones. Would anyone try to walk any distance in them?"

"Thanks Alan, have you noticed my soft shoe shuffle yet? they would be ideal."

So she has a sense of humour, I liked that. "Perhaps we can find a jazz club, and have a night out all of us."

"Like the sarcasm," muttered Patrick. "How do you know we can dance, I did once try the River Dance that all those Irish clodhoppers were good at."

"And did you win them over?" Terry asked.

"No my trousers were too tight."

Jasmine laughed and said "Great fellas, keep up the good work, we might need a laugh or two before we're done. Lets get back in the car and move along a bit. I've got to arrange somewhere for us to bed down for the night."

CHAPTER 14

We gently woke Yasmin and her sons. They seemed totally lost for a few minutes, then she said "Thank you for letting us sleep, that was the most comfortable night I've had in ages." she smiled as she said it. She asked if we had any drinking water, which Jasmine produced for her, and then said. "You had better soon start looking out for your husband now, as we are catching up with the refugees again."

We all stared at the moving humanity that was drifting alongside the road. I didn't notice any fathers carrying children any more, I guess the weight was getting them down. We carried on slowly for about four miles, Yasmin searching the faces as we went. Jasmine meanwhile had been looking at a detailed map she had and she said, "I think we can find a hotel in the next town. It's about another sixty miles. Is that ok Terry?"

"Sure," he said, "the sooner we catch up with Yasmin's husband the better though, then we can start our programme. Will you book a family room for our guests as well."

"Of course, and I will ensure they can provide us with a packed lunch, or whatever they have that's suitable."

"Good idea, did you get anything from our last hotel?"

"Yes, it's in a warming bag in the boot. We have some

pizza, I'll get it when we next stop."

We were now driving along a road going through some rolling hills, very rocky on the coastal side. There were fields on the other side and I saw cows, also sheep and I was surprised to see quite a good growth of grass. Jasmine meanwhile was talking in Turkish to, I guess, the hotel of her choice. She seemed to be a bit bothered by the response, and it took some minutes before she switched her mobile off.

She then said "Terry that was difficult, It's a so called three star Turkish hotel but, they have a very limited meal for tonight. They have had some trouble with electricity, and their freezer has to be replaced, Shall I try elsewhere? This one is recommended, but we don't want to start with a food problem, They can accommodate us all, but can't guarantee an evening meal."

"Is there a restaurant close by?" asked Terry.

"No not very close. I did ask that very question."

"Try somewhere else then."

"OK," and she got out the map and a handbook.

Within a couple of minutes she was deep in conversation again, when Terry suddenly asked Amil to stop. He got out of the car and crossed the road to a tall turbaned man, we saw him introduce himself and they had a conversation. Terry was nodding for some time as the man talked to him. This went on for a few minutes until Terry shook his hand, and came back to the car.

"That was one of the Turks plants walking with the refugees, he says he has his eye on a group of three youngish men that are a little ahead of him. He is concerned by their actions and has asked for some back up to question them. We should be around in case they want any of it filmed, the only problem is, it would mean exposing us. But then they may still think we are just making a documentary. Keep the speed right down Amil, lets travel at the same pace as the procession."

This is getting exciting I thought, what if they are terrorists, will they be carrying guns or bombs? I then started to worry a bit, what is Patrick and Amil doing, they are both still acting exactly as they have been before, just calmly moving along with us in the car. Did I expect Patrick to pull out a gun or something, and, where does Amil keep his?

I studied them both, Patrick was keeping an eye on the little group around the turbaned man, I looked a little ahead, and sure enough, there were three youngish guys, and they all had back packs. Two of them had small beards, the third was clean shaven. They didn't appear to be mixing with any of those around them, and walked in a line together.

Yasmin meanwhile was keeping a watchful eye on all the refugees, neither of her sons had uttered a word since we left the charity table. I wondered what they were thinking in this situation. I made myself a promise, I would chat to them when we had resolved the three young guys. I also wondered if they had any games to play. I know my sisters son of six loved his games, and playing make believe, maybe the long hours of walking, the pressure with their father not being with them, and the conversations going on around them, was affecting them. Yasmin had said they were both passable in English, so they would have understood what was going on.

Jasmine suddenly interrupted my thinking. "OK everyone we have a hotel in Alanya, it's on the coast, so we might get a glimpse of the sea. They can feed us and sleep us, and you will all be pleased to know that there is a bit of a spar, so if we have the time for a sauna, it might be possible."

"That's great" Terry said, "did you give them any arrival time, cos we may be stuck with this lot for a while."

"No, I said we couldn't be there for a while as we were travelling slowly with some refugees."

"Fine" as he said this his mobile rang, he said, "Amil go

about a hundred yards and stop. Dan get the camera ready to start filming, you help Patrick, make it look like you are just filming all the walkers. The back-up is arriving, they will pull out the three guys. Our man will just carry on as a refugee. Alan get your camera ready, you act as a back-up for Dan."

We all got ready to jump out of the car and seconds later Amil stopped, he got out as well, he spoke to Yasmin, telling her to keep in the car I guess, as she nodded and said something to her sons. Dan quickly set up his hand held camera. Patrick stood alongside him with his sound box and mike on a pole. Terry stopped a couple of walkers and asked if they spoke English? One of them nodded and Terry asked him where he was from, and had he had a difficult journey. As the man started to answer there were some shouts from the following crowd, and I watched four heavily armed police pull out the three that were under suspicion. The rest of the refugees stopped and stared, whilst the police questioned them. Voices were raised and some pulling and waving of arms from the three guys.

Terry said, "switch to them Dan."

"Ok but they are a bit far away to be very effective."

"Can you get nearer?"

"Sure," with that he and Patrick walked nearer to the scuffle, filming as he did so...I followed on and when they stopped I went past and started taking photos.

One of the police turned on me and waved me away, pointing at our car and shouting, "car, car", I had no idea what he was saying, but he just kept pulling my arm and pointing at our car, so I slowly backed off. He did the same to Dan and Patrick, the other police were still questioning the suspects, but gradually the volume went down, and whatever had passed was not too worrying. The three opened their back packs, the police looked into them, then pushed them back to join the staring refugees.

Dan then made a show of filming them as they started walking again. One of the policemen came up to Terry, who now had Jasmine standing beside him, asked him a question, Jasmine answered I guess, telling him that we were making a documentary of the situation and after some minutes of talking, he shook Terry's hand and the four of them got back into their car, and drove off. We packed everything back into the boot of the car and climbed in.

Terry said "They are dressed as police but are in effect part of the Turkish Special Forces. They are aware of what we are doing, but put on a bit of a show herding us back to the car. Apparently the young guys are part of a Syrian football team and are just as desperate to get away, as are all the others."

I found it all intriguing and fascinating. This was James Bond stuff, and great experience for a Norfolk lad, as I liked to call myself. I should have some good stories to tell when I get back to civilisation.

Jasmine got out a blue bag from the boot and carried it into the car. "We have pizza everyone, Its already cut, and you can hold it in the serviettes." It was still a bit warm and we all tucked in, the two boys were both smiling as they ate.

Amil got us cruising again, Yasmin concentrated on the walking groups. The pattern didn't change, just a toiling group of people walking, walking, walking, to where? Most of them were just staring ahead, some had their heads bowed, either in concentration, or perhaps praying. Some bent with exhaustion, and, the odd few conversing. It was a sorry sight, and we must all have been affected, because we were also totally quiet for some time, with Terry and Yasmin both concentrating on their prospective jobs.

We came across another long charity table, where there were many sitting or lying around the area. Yasmin asked

Amil to stop and she, without any bidding from Terry, got out of the car and stood gazing at the mass of humanity. She walked along a little, both her boys were looking anxiously out of the windows, after a little while she returned and said. "He doesn't appear to be there anywhere."

She looked very sad and downcast, but hugged both her sons and we continued, Amil now saying. "We probably have another ten or so miles to go to our stopover, but I guess we will take some time at this pace."

No one commented and we moved on. I looked at what we were travelling through. There were patches of green mainly on the countryside, some houses, a few trees, but nothing to get too excited about. The coastal side was quite rocky, with the occasional rough lane, probably wide enough for a car to get down. We caught the odd glimpse of sea but, there was generally a feeling of desolation. Probably when we got to Alanya we might see some tourist attractions, and a bit of Turkish life.

Inwardly I was looking forward to getting there, my heart wasn't really in driving along at virtually a walking pace, and the sooner we caught up with Yasmin's husband the better. We still had quite a distance before we got to Fethiya. Having looked at Jasmine's map, after Antalya, we then had to go inland for some miles. as it was some way further on when Turkey, and the Greek islands got closer together. Some of the TV reports I had seen back in England, said that at Lesbos, you could plainly see the Turkish coast.

We carried on through some pretty dusty and dry areas, with very little beauty, this upset me a bit. I remembered when I went to Turunc, it was absolutely beautiful countryside, undulating, very green and mountainous. But, that was a holiday resort, this is very much a road between small towns.

We were still travelling at a very slow pace when Yasmin

suddenly bounced up and down on her seat, told Amil to stop, she had seen the man travelling with her husband. She leapt out and pushed her way into a group that was standing looking at something in their midst. I then saw her wrapping her arms around a man that was well dressed compared to many of the refugees. Suddenly both boys excitedly started shouting what I guess was daddy, and they both looked longingly at the door. Terry opened it for them and they raced out and flung themselves onto the man. He looked up at us as he caressed Yasmin and the boys. She was talking excitedly and pointing at us. Then all four of them came over to the car. He was pulling a travel case, and had a back pack, obviously loaded with their belongings.

Terry stepped out and shook hands with the man. I heard him say welcome, then Jasmine also got out and greeted them in Syrian I guess. He didn't look at all as I had imagined, he was not very tall, had quite long brown hair going a little grey, thin on top, rimless glasses, and a few days growth of beard, but when he smiled, which he was doing as his two boys clung on to him, his face lit up.

Amil got out of the car and also greeted him in his own language. He turned to some of the refugees that were just standing staring at the warm exchanges that were going on. One of them was very tall and towered over the rest of them. Yasmin's husband was shaking hands with some six or seven people he had been walking with, and, as he spoke he gestured towards the car and Patrick suddenly commented, "He should be able to give us some up to date news on the situation for them all."

Dan grunted to this and added, "I think we need to have a very full discussion with her husband, before we enter into any sort of agreement with him and his family."

Terry and Jasmine came back to the car, Yasmin and her husband followed, the boys were staring at the tall man and saying something I couldn't understand, then they followed and climbed in. Terry introduced him to us, his name was Hussain. He shook hands with each of us, and said in fairly good English, "I am delighted to meet you, thank you for caring for my wife and children. They have constantly been on my mind, and only after I had gone some miles, did I realise just how dangerous it could have been for them all; I almost turned back but, Yasmin gave me strict instructions to get well ahead, make good time as she would eventually catch up. Now being able to ride with you is so comforting. So thank you all. If there is anything I can help with please let me know. Are you all in good health?"

We all grunted yes.

"I have been in touch with friends who are much further north than us, they are finding difficulty in acquiring transport to Greece, they are in Fethiye, which is where some of them had been directed but, most of the refugees are now going much further north, where the Greek islands are much closer to Turkey. who now is providing some tented camps for us all, as they feared that it may get quite cold in the next two or three months."

This was quite a speech and he stopped and squeezed Yasmin's hand. We started to travel at a reasonable speed, everyone was quiet, Yasmin and her family were sitting in the third row whilst I sat with Patrick and Dan, it was good to get moving. I had spent so much time gazing at the refugees that I hadn't really been taking in what the country had to offer. We had been on the main coastal road most of the time. I asked Jasmine if I could borrow the map. Whilst we had been level we were now going through undulating rocky countryside, and I could see a long mountain range running northwards. The map said Tase Yalas, Jasmine assured me it's, 'Taurus Mountains'. There were a few houses and the odd café along our road but very light on people. I had not really taken in if other traffic was using the road, now it was quite busy.

I said to Patrick, "Its amazing how you can travel as we have, and not really see anything other than that directly in front of your eyes. I have been totally concentrated on the refugees and there's a whole world out there, if our stop this evening is at all interesting, how about savouring a bit of local colour?"

"I can't think why not, unless Terry has something for us to do."

"Well we can try, I must say, it's been all work and no play so far, I wouldn't mind a bit of life be it in a bar or whatever."

"Me too, and I know dashing Dan wouldn't mind a bit of freedom, would you senor?"

"Yea indeed my slave."

Jasmine turned to us, she was sitting in the front with Terry and Amil, "What are you guys planning? you know we have guests to take care of."

Terry said, "I suggest we all meet in the bar if they have one, and then we can get down to discussing our next moves, we can travel at a proper pace now, and get some distance during the day. I think we still have a long way to go before we get to the embarkation areas. Maybe Hussain will be ready to fill us in with what's required."

Jasmin said, "Yes he will be ready with whatever news he has." With that she spoke to him in their own language.

I noticed that Jasmine turned her head a little to pick up what was being said. It was just a noise to me. At times we would drive for some minutes, and not see any refugees, then there would be perhaps another group some fifty yards long. We also passed another stopping area with two long tables set up and the usual groups of travellers sitting or lying around them.

CHAPTER 15

Amil suddenly said. "We will soon be in Alanya, It's a very old town, fortified and with a history that could make your blood curdle." He laughed as he said that. "But, its modernised to some extent, it has a great rock as a buttress. Used to be one of the main ports for Turkey but, is not used much today. Do you want me to drive around a bit before we settle in the hotel?"

We all looked at Terry, who said. "No, let's get to the hotel, unload, settle in then have a meet. If any of you want to look around the town afterwards that's ok, but, we have quite a distance to go before we get to the launching places, so don't want to be late away tomorrow morning."

No one answered that, and I noticed the coastal scenery was changing rapidly as we approached the town. For the last few miles we had been travelling through sparsely inhabited areas, probably fishing villages. There were some headland forests, one or two fiords, and yet on the inland side there had been a flat area, obviously used for farming. Not now though as we got nearer, the terrain was rocky. It also appeared to have a fortress wall around the bit of the town I could see. Certainly the town looked as if it was set on rock, or had been built incorporating the sloping rocks, and there was quite a drop towards what must be the harbour.

Jasmine, her notebook opened, directed Amil to the hotel. We drove through two large pillars, some ten feet high, there was a gravel type semi-circular entrance, and a small car park off to the left. Amil stopped in front of the main reception door, and we all piled out. It looked a little foreboding, with quite old stonework on the front walls, very little vegetation and a fairly run down entrance hall.

Jasmine said "This was originally used as a guard house and prison, that's way back of course, but has recently, well since the tourist business has grown in Turkey, been transformed into a hotel and if my information here is correct, they have a bit of a spa somewhere."

The reception area was spacious, a very serious looking man was behind the long desk, he was joined by a beautiful dark skinned youngish girl. Patrick and I headed for her, she gave us a wide smile and booked us in then, pointed out the dining room. We thanked her. Terry and Jasmine were also headed towards a lift. A lift, that must be a message that the hotel was well appointed.

I went back to the girl and asked her where the spa was, she looked a bit confused then answered. "Well it's a small gym, a plunge pool and a hot tub outside at the rear, the door is to the left of the lift." I thanked her as she tended to Yasmin, her husband, and children.

Terry stopped at the lift and said to us all. "Let's meet in half an hour in the sitting room area."

I arrived at my room, it was quite spacious, a double bed, a wide window overlooking some small trees which looked like banana plants, could it be? There was also quite a view of the mountains behind us, all very acceptable. I was also amused to see a large chess board carved into the garden area, with some figures on it, white and black, and big. That should appeal to Terry I thought. My room had an on suite bathroom with a shower over the bath, I was surprised to see a bidet, now that was something. I guess the owners were either French or German, as I recall someone saying that this area was very popular with holidaymakers. I wondered if I could get a reception for my telephone, I hadn't given it much thought for two days and on switching it on found I had some texts. The first one was from Rachel, and she was worried. The message said that yesterday, two men had arrived and wanted to look over the premises. When asked why, they said that I was under scrutiny by our government, and they had been tasked with finding out what sort of work I did, and in particular, had I been working in Turkey or Greece. She had said that as far as she knew, I had never worked in either country.

They had seemed content with that and had left her. What's it all about Alan? was the end of her message.

The second was from .Kevin, my director friend from Nice. He wanted to know when I would be available for the Serbia programme. He was at present doing some background study on the job there. I wondered, dare I say in two weeks time. Everything here seemed to be planned for a two week stint. I decided that I would make it three weeks, and gave him a date. Told him I was in Turkey but didn't add anything on what I was doing.

The third message was from Karen, my ex Australian model girlfriend. She had been offered work in Berlin and Paris, and wondered if I was interested in meeting up again. It was in a month. I considered that, perhaps it would also tie in with Maria. I answered, told her I was in Turkey on a job and would be delighted to meet up, let me know the actual dates and where you will be staying. I finished it with a couple of kisses, well you never know.

I had a quick wash and brush up, then went down to the bar. Terry was already there with Jasmine. As I came out of the lift, Yasmin and her family came down the stairs and joined us. Terry ordered a bottle of white wine, two beers, for Dan and Patrick I assumed, and fruit juices for Yasmin and her boys. She told them to play outside, because they both dutifully went out of the back sliding door on to a patio that led to the large chess set there.

Terry led us to a sitting room alongside the dining room. Dan and Patrick arrived as we started, they picked up their beers and we all sat around Terry. He said, "I've had news that there has been trouble at one of the embarkation areas around Fethiye, it was quietened by the Turkish Police. They tried to arrest some traffickers, and a bit of a battle took place, consequently most of the traffickers are now believed to be much further north, some as far as Bodrum. That's some two hundred miles from here. I had wanted to get to Antalya tomorrow, some hundred miles, but, we should go on quite a bit further, on the quicker inland road, I can't think that Yasmin and her family would get any opportunity to find passages from any of the small ports along the coastal road."

He was quite convincing in his appraisal of the situation. Yasmin and Hussain seemed quite assured by his views and she, speaking for them both said. "We are so grateful for taking us so far and we will fit in with your suggestions. So yes please."

"Terry then said, tomorrow we will start reasonably early, get as far as possible and take a break around lunch time for us oldies and our young ones can run around a bit. We may also pass, or see some of the camps that Turkey is setting up. Now Yasmin, if your husband would talk us through what he envisages for you, and how he would like to handle your travel arrangements."

He first of all thanked us, saying. "What a boost we had given him and his family with our kindness and concern.

When we knew we were going to leave Aleppo we spent some time deciding on what our real aim was, bearing in mind our careers. We thought about getting to Turkey, possibly hiring a car and driving through Europe to Germany, where we feel our talents would be appreciated. When we were ready to set off we thought of driving our car to the border, leaving it, and joining the rest of the refugees. Maybe hitchhiking a bit but, with a family of four, that would limit our chances. We knew one company that traded in fruit and vegetables, which they transported to various countries. We made contact with one particular driver that I had treated a year or so ago, he was pleased to help, he gave strict instructions on where to be at a certain time. He also had some more people getting out of Syria.

We spread ourselves around his lorry, lying alongside his load, and in the children's cases, on top of his load. Luckily we were not stopped, and after many miles, at times very uncomfortable, we were dropped just outside Kas. From there we started walking, also trying to get lifts from cars and lorries, but with no success. It was then that Yasmin insisted on me hurrying ahead, as the children were both exhausted. The rest you know. We are happy to be used for your documentary, and will help wherever we can, but, when we get to a sizable town, I would like to explore the possibility of hiring a car and driving ourselves. We have both been made aware of the dangers of sea travel. I have talked to several people travelling with me and the most worrying aspect is that many of them are professional land-owning, business operating, engineers, professors, teachers and shop keepers. As so many of them have, like us, got out of the turmoil, the infrastructure of the country will collapse."

Terry thanked him for his appraisal of the situation, then said. "I don't know what the chances are of you hiring a car here, presumably it would have to be cash? What is the situation in Syria re using credit cards, or banking cheques?"

"It was so desperate back at home that you couldn't trust any news that came out. Also a great deal of stealing and misuse of identities was going on. For the last two or three months, there was no payment in the hospitals. Initially I was on Assad's side, but as everything deteriorated, my feelings changed, but, it's such a mixture of groups all fighting for their particular ends, that it is impossible now in Syria, and even if Russia increases its support for Assad, I cannot see this war ending for some considerable time. Diplomacy will not work whilst the various factions are there, and, if Assad does drive them out, where will they go? Remember there is a rag bag army in Syria, they could just as easily descend on any of the bordering countries and then what will happen?"

His long speech made us all think, This man, a doctor, who is trained in serving people is most likely representing the views of many of the displaced people, and finding somewhere that will welcome him is going to be very difficult.

Terry said, "thanks again, you have given us much to think about. Now, tomorrow is going to be a long drive, so I suggest we have dinner in say half an hour and maybe an early night." He looked at me as he said this, perhaps he heard me talk to Patrick earlier. Is he playing mother?

CHAPTER 16

We set off early, and quickly made good progress. Terry seemed to have given up looking for Turkish Special Services people, although he was sitting in the window seat. The refugees seemed to be much lighter in numbers as we neared Antalya. I had a slight hangover as I had spent a while last evening with Patrick and Dan, looking at Alanya. We had found a bar, set over a promontory that dominated the town, and though it was dark, the scene was superb, well lit, all the way down to the harbour. The owner of the bar spoke a bit of English, he said there were two wonderful beaches to the right, and the town was now very much a tourist destination.

We got to Antalya fairly quickly. Amil said we had, but by-passing on a ring road.

Terry said, "We are taking the 350 road which winds a bit through the mountains, but is much closer to Fethiye than going by the coast road."

No one responded. The countryside was magnificent with great rolling mountains and as we climbed at some of the bends we would get a glimpse of the sea. After a short while Amil said. "We shall soon be in Korkuteli, a small town very colourful". As we passed through, it seemed strange not to see refugees.

When we had nearly cleared the town Terry suggested we stop at a drive in and fairly large café.

"Perhaps some of you would like a rest room." He said this with a smile, that was intended for Yasmin and her family. Terry saying rest room. I winked at Patrick and he nodded. "Olde English gent."

We all piled into the café, it was pretty simple in design with brown wooden tables spread throughout.

Very few customers. Yasmin and her two children went off through a curtain and we all sat round a long table, A tired looking man wearing an apron with a picture of a footballer on it, came over and asked what we wanted in Turkish. Jasmine asked for a menu. The waiter wiped his hands on his apron and wandered back to the bar. It was beers all round, apart from Yasmin and her boys, we all trooped in turn into the 'rest room' and Jasmine ordered a vegetarian lunch of humus and flat bread, a bit of salad, and we were soon ready to start again.

Amil was making very good time when Terry's telephone buzzed, he answered it and he said "around five o'clock, where, OK." Then he asked Jasmine to arrange a hotel in Fethiye, near the main harbour.

She got out her map and note book then telephoned. She talked for some minutes in Turkish, then said.

"We are ok, maybe not too luxurious, but they have beds and food. Plus, we can see the sea, that will appeal to Alan."

I pretended to cry and wailed, "How can I retain my figure without exercise?"

"Well you could run behind the car for a few miles," She answered.

"Thanks, but could we wait until we get near our destination, and its downhill."

"Are you serious?" She said.

"If I can wear my spring heeled stilts yes."

That got a laugh and Dan grunting "Maybe I should join you, I'm feeling in need of some fun and fat isn't fun."

Jasmine took it all in good part and said, "fellas you all look in good trim, if I was a young girl you would turn my head, and no doubt all lead me astray."

"Yes" we all shouted. It suddenly occurred to me, most of our time had been pretty serious, no doubt influenced by the state of the refugees.

"How much longer do you reckon?" Terry asked Amil.

"About an hour."

"Great, are we all ok for not stopping till we get there?"

We all muttered a bit, but no-one needed the rest room!!

I turned round and asked Yasmin how the boys were doing?

"I have never been so impressed with their quietness. At home they were always dashing around, kicking a football, climbing a tree we had in our garden, and generally being active. I'm sure they will be ready to run around when we get to the hotel."

I asked the oldest. "Which football team do you support in Syria?"

He looked a bit embarrassed and said in good English. "The Syrian team, we have some very good footballers in our team, many of them play around the world in other leagues, but, the war has stopped that, we've not had an international match for some time now."

I was very impressed by his answer.

"What position do you play?"

"Left wing."

"Are you what we call in England, 'a leftie.'"

He didn't know what to say to that, and turned to his father with a look of anticipation.

"I think he's ambidextrous," said his father.

"That's good" I said, "and what about your other one, does he like football?"

"Oh yes, but he's defence."

Both the boys sat up a bit straighter and were all smiles – we had communicated.

Terry interrupted with, "I'm getting in touch with the Turkish Special Services to see what the situation is now. but I think it will help us all if we can get a lead on any trafficking that is still taking place there after the so called battle."

No one answered, that seemed to be good policy.

Amil decided to sing a bit in Turkish, that helped us all with the heaviness of fast constant driving, a bit later he said ."We should be there in about fifteen minutes. Fethiye has one of the most beautiful harbours in the whole of western Turkey, there is a lovely bay, on the eastern side of a gulf. It's an ancient town set in the foot of some rugged mountains, some of which we have been through.

When we are in the town if you look back towards the mountains you can see many caves or tombs, as they were known, carved into the rocks. These have been there for centuries and just outside the town hall is a sarcophagus, mounted on a high stone pediment, all done to worship the dead I guess."

"I take it you've been a few times?" Terry asked, "sounds fascinating, are there many shops near the harbour, I wondered if they were ones that were selling faulty wet suits and life jackets."

"There are some, but mostly in the town, you will see when we get to the harbour."

We entered the town and started winding downhill, we were all somewhat excited about the possibility of seeing and meeting traffickers, and all that might develop. I'm sure that Yasmin and Hussain are getting anxious about their immediate future.

CHAPTER 17

The hotel was set back from the harbour, with a large parking area alongside, we all got out, stretched a bit. Terry and Jasmine, with their small cases, led us to the main door of the hotel. Amil suggested it might be wise for us to take our equipment in as the car was fully exposed, and there was no gate or any obvious security cameras, Dan and Patrick took theirs, I pulled my own out of the car, struggled with it and my case to the door.

There was a splendid reception area, with a large fish tank in the centre, full of small, highly coloured fish. There were several chairs, with a dark brown tone, even two arm chairs. There were no other guests to be seen and we had the attention of two middle aged smiling ladies.

They quickly arranged our rooms and Jasmine talked to them as we booked in. One of the ladies called out, and a young boy arrived, he was to help me with my equipment. I wondered. Do I tip him? Then realised I still had no money, must talk to Jasmine about that. I should be able to get some from a bank if I used my credit card. I dropped everything in the room, hardly giving it a glance, although I did notice that a light was on beside the bed, then went back down to reception. I asked one of the ladies if she would call Jasmine,

When she answered, I asked her if I would be able to change some money in a bank. She said of course, they may well still be open, remember, this is the continent. I asked the lady that spoke English if there was a bank close to us.

She thought for a few seconds then glanced at her wrist and said. "It will still be open." She gave me instructions where to go, then added, "most of the people there speak good English."

I set off, following her instructions, and saw a large group of refugees, some in smaller groups, others either single or with a family. Many were congregated around what appeared to be a stage in a square. I heard raised voices, and as I stood still and watched. There was much pushing and shouting at two men that were being raised onto the stage, which was in front of a wall. This had an enormous free painting on it. Ah Banksy, I thought, street art. The voices got even louder and sounded angry. I wonder if this is a trafficker situation. Wish I had brought my camera. As I stood there on the edge of the crowd we suddenly had a line of police surging down towards the demonstrators, some had batons drawn.

I stepped back a few paces trying to avoid being involved in the rush, but I was too slow. I was pushed from behind and found myself wedged in with all the refugees. Children were crying mothers trying to quieten them, and the two people on the platform were being hauled down by the police. They had driven a line through the refugees to get to the two men. More police were arriving, and then a siren wailed, and a black maria arrived. The two men were frog marched through the refugees and thrown into the van.

I couldn't have used my camera anyway as we were all crushed together. There was no-one I could talk too, not knowing one word of Turkish. I tried to ease my way out of the crowd. It was slow going and they seemed to want to vent their anger at anyone, as some fights were breaking out among them. Then I heard a crash of glass, across the street, some young refugees were breaking into a clothing shop and running off with things. The police turned their attention to them and batons were now being used, screams echoing around the street. Another black maria arrived with a clanging horn and flashing blue light. The young thieves that had been caught, were being pushed and hit on their legs to drive them into the van.

I saw the whole episode, realising that we had been totally unaware of the real problems of the refugees, Our passage to here had been quite painless. All those that were trying to get to the traffickers were desperate.

Two of the police got on to the platform and they shouted instructions to the crowd I guess. I wish I had knowledge of Turkish, because as they talked the crowd started to disperse. I managed to get out of the crowd and started walking following my instructions towards the bank. When I arrived the doors were shut, I couldn't get any reply to my knocking. I wondered if the disturbance had caused an early closure. I trudged back to the hotel and went to my room. I felt quite depressed from my experience. Then I thought, how must the refugees feel, they will have walked for days, maybe weeks or months. Presumably, the two traffickers represented hope for them.

I had a shower, changed, and went down to reception. Terry was there with Jasmine. She was talking to the lady at the desk, Terry went into the street outside. I asked Jasmine what was happening.

She said. "Terry has a meeting with his contact at the Security Services, then we might get some news on what our next move will be."

I told her of my experience, she reacted quietly and said when I had finished. "Alan, I did say earlier that we would have difficulties when we get to the actual places of departure. I have been talking to the manager of the hotel. He said the police have really worked hard on capturing the traffickers recently. Particularly, as the Turkish news each day, has been talking about their reaction. Various political people in Europe have been scathing in their comments about the freedom that traffickers seem to have here. Because of this, police activity has increased, and driven most of them much further north. So I guess it means we have more driving to get to the departure places, and they said that many of the refugees are travelling as far as Bodrum, and beyond, because of its proximity to Greek Islands."

"What about Yasmin and her family, have you talked to them yet?"

"No, but will as soon as they come down here."

"Have you not seen them at all?"

"I expect they're resting, a bed must be heaven for them all after their weeks of travel."

"No doubt Hussain will want to look around here tomorrow, to see if he can hire a car, or see any traffickers do you think?"

"Probably but we don't want to spend too much time here, unless Terry has other ideas after his meeting."

CHAPTER 18

Jasmine called me in my room and said, "It's strange Alan. Terry's been gone for nearly two hours and not phoned through, or left any messages. When he went out he said, should be back in an hour."

"Well it may be more important to spend time with his contacts, I wouldn't worry too much."

"Thanks Alan, but can't help it, not like him to be vague about time."

"And have you seen Yasmin and her family?"

"No not at all."

"Jasmine I'll come down, are you in your room, or at the reception area?"

"I'm at reception."

I went down, she was there talking to a man. The manager of the hotel I guessed. She left him and came to me "It's time to eat, will you call Patrick and Dan. I will wander out a bit and have a look round, but will call Yasmin first."

I saw her on the house phone, looking mystified, then she came over to me and said. "Yasmin and her boys are in the family room, but her husband has been out for nearly two hours, and she is worried about him."

"Maybe he's with Terry looking around."

"Maybe, hadn't thought of that." Yasmin and her boys arrived,

I phoned Patrick first, to tell him dinner was ready, he said. "I've got Dan here, we'll be down in a jiffy." All eight of us sat and we talked through dinner. At the end still no sign of Terry or Hussain. Jasmine was now getting despondent.

"I don't know how we can get in touch, I've tried his mobile, it's on message only."

"He didn't give you any names, or numbers then?"

"No."

"There's not much we can do, not knowing where he is or what's happened, but, that also applies to Hussain. I know Yasmin is very anxious."

Dan says, "Let's go hunt around the town a bit, see if there are any groups, or anything that might point to him being involved."

We all agreed. Then just as we were about to go out of the door, in walks Terry and Hussain, chatting as they come.

Yasmin threw her arms around her husband, he looked a bit uncomfortable but returned her hug, then gently pushed her away a bit and exclaimed cheerfully. "We are unlikely to get any shipment from here, and I cannot hire a car. We, Terry and I, have tried several outlets for the car and no one will allow it. So Terry, will explain our other result."

Terry said, "I'm sorry if we worried you, it's taken hours to get any real information. My contact told me that there is very little, if any trafficking from here now. The police have tightened their activities and, were able to arrest just a few initially, the rest have gone much further up the coast. The police are trying to keep an eye on the traffickers, but, when they arrest one, another takes their place. And, they are worried, because there is definitely a big organisation behind their activities. They have some suspicions but, apparently there are a few sources of finance, and even though they had commandeered many boats, more seem to appear, and most of the starts are at night now. So whilst they are patrolling much of the coastline, it is so diverse and spread out, that it is impossible to keep everything under control."

Jasmine asked. "So what are our plans?"

"We leave tomorrow as early as possible and aim either for Bodrum, or what's known as, the end of the Dorian peninsular, both fairly close to some of the Greek islands."

"Terry, we have all eaten, I'm sure the hotel will knock something up for you." Hussain talked to Yasmin in their language, then the two of them went into the dining room. We, Dan, Patrick, Jasmine, and Amil shuffled around a bit, so I suggested a bottle of wine, beer of course for the real men...and whatever for Amil...It was easily agreed. We were all relieved that the two of them had appeared. Jasmine said she wanted some time alone with Terry, to get a more detailed account of what had happened, and why he had spent so much time with Hussain. We then settled into the main bar area.

We set off early the next morning. Jasmin said over breakfast that she had talked to Terry and they had decided to go to Knidos, right at the tip of the Dorian peninsular, and very easy for crossings to three Greek islands. It was some miles past Marmaris, and she thought about two hundred miles in total, so it would be a five hour drive at least. We were all pretty sanguine about that, and I think, all wanting to see some real action. Maybe Hussain and Yasmin might view it differently, but talking to Patrick and Dan They were both somewhat bored with sitting and driving, so not much conversation floated around the car. Amil occasionally sang to us a bit. I had borrowed the map from Jasmine and was particularly interested to see we would be passing quite close to Dalaman, where I had flown on my holiday previously. I wondered if the storks were still in evidence, and when I mentioned this, Dan said "You were in a haze of love then and I bet they were a dream, as you no doubt thought they would inspire your Aussie girl friend to be nice to you."

"She was 'nice' to me anyway. When you are handsome and intelligent, these things happen Dan. Perhaps I could give you the odd lesson."

"Some chance" he growled, "but, I'm willing to wager a few lira that we won't see any."

"OK, how much for each stork?"

"Twenty, and if we don't see any you pay me one hundred." I thought about that, what if it had been a particular time of the year. But lira, don't know how much they are worth.

"OK, you're on."

It gave us all something to look for, although Yasmin nor Hussain seemed very interested, but the two boys started peering out excitedly.

The countryside was changing quite rapidly from mile to mile, then when we were passing the Dalaman area. it was built up and suddenly the oldest boy shouted. "Look there are two on that tall building." Sure enough there were two storks, sitting at the top of a very tall square building that looked like a viewing station for aircraft, but couldn't be. It was too far away from the airport.

"Hey Dan, things looking up."

"I'm still well in pocket," he replied, but not for long because Patrick suddenly did the same thing.

"Look at The Mosque. There's one there."

In the next four or five miles, whilst we went through the villages and built up area, we saw another seven, before we were again travelling through country.

"Dan I will let you off, just buy me a gin and tonic if and

when we find a bar tonight."

"OK, but you were lucky."

Terry suddenly chirped up "I suggest we stop at the next village or town, if we see a likely bar or restaurant."

We all agreed, we had been travelling for at least three hours. Yasmin said, "I would like to give the boys a little run somewhere, before we settle in to eating."

CHAPTER 19

We ate mainly in silence, then returned to the car. After travelling for another two hours, Amil informed us we were approaching Knidos, We had passed Marmaris earlier, where the side of the road was lightly occupied with a few refugees, some helping others that were obviously suffering from sore feet, and maybe injuries. There were also more children, some seemed to be in little groups, without parents, others clinging onto a helping hand. There was very little conversation, they were all walking to what they would term, freedom.

Our next hotel turned out to be quite big, fairly modern in outlook with several cars parked in front and to the side. After booking in, we all met, and Terry told us that, we should be able to film in areas around a small harbour, where apparently boats set off for Greece. He suggested to Hussain that he comes with our film crew, and try to organise their departure.

Hussain said Yasmin and the boys should stay in the hotel, until he had arranged their transport. We now had a plan, and we might get to work on it.

Dan and Patrick checked out their equipment. I did the same, and we set off. The hotel manager directed us to the harbour. He assured us it was but a few minutes walk. Jasmine and Amil came with us, he carrying a small man bag, I suddenly thought. Of course, he is our security.

We passed a few shops and following our instructions, turned into a small narrow lane, at the end we were confronted with a mass of refugees. Most of them were milling about, no doubt wanting the same as Hussain, someone to deal with... Terry suggested that we, Dan, Patrick, and me, were to set up the camera across from where we were standing, alongside the small harbour. He would mix with the refugees with Hussain and Amil, and see if they could find someone to deal with. He then wanted to bring them to where we were, and we could film them with Hussain. Jasmine, who had been quiet until then said, "Terry are you sure this is the best way to deal with it, wouldn't it be better if the boys were with you and filmed the initial contact, as I'm sure it will be very difficult to do it the way you're suggesting."

"Jasmine, I think it will be very cumbersome for us all to push our way through and, I think Hussain and I have a better chance to find who we want, if there are just the two of us. I'm sure that if we can trace any traffickers, once they have seen the colour of Hussain's money, they will be more likely to want to keep their nasty fingers on it. But, let's see what reception we get, and keep our minds set on our objective. Amil can do any translation with Hussain. I have to meet my opposite number here, he said it was important that I was brought up to date on Turkey's situation regarding the refugees. So, I will see you in a little while. I will take Hussain initially and help him if I can." With that they went off together.

I could see both points of view, it was a tricky situation and I thought we would be lucky if it was fruitful. They walked off in the direction of the harbour entrance, going alongside the biggest crush of refugees. Jasmine came beside me, and she looked worried. "You made a good point," I said.

"I can't see how we can get round what must be secrecy with the traffickers. They must be on their guard, if it's true that the police are rounding them up. Yet every day more and more refugees are getting to Greece, according to the news, either on TV or in the papers. I'm also looking up what I can every night on my iPad and telephone."

We had a few curious refugees taking an interest in Dan's mounted camera, three young boys started acting out a scene in front of him. He responded by giving them a huge smile and a pat on the head for the biggest one.

They kept saying something that sounded like, tellywelly, and laughing as they did so. Then Jasmine asked them a question and the oldest answered her. They had a conversation for a couple of minutes. He kept pointing towards the harbour entrance. She eventually finished her discussion with a big kiss, which she threw at them with her hand. They ran off, I guess to find their parents, and she said, "I asked them where they were going, and when. They said their parents were with someone that was sailing with them to an island, that's all they knew."

"Maybe it's worth trying to find them with their parents, that might be a lead into who they are dealing with."

"OK Alan, let's see if we can find them. Will you wait here?" she asked the other two.

"Yep, that's fine by us," says Dan.

We walked quickly in the same direction as the young boys. "Jasmine, is this a wild goose chase, as we say in narfulk?"

She gave me an old fashioned look, "Alan, this is it really, we know from the info that Terry has been given that several recent sailings have gone from here. It's up to us to investigate every possible outlet to see if we can come up with anything."

There were several small groups of refugees huddled together, as we walked quickly down the slope towards the harbour. It was still reasonably warm. It was a small town, very scruffy in the area that we were walking through, various papers, the odd cardboard box, clothes just discarded in lumps strewn along in front of a run-down shop. I guess some sleeping places. As we got nearer the harbour, there were three quite large rubber dinghies moored alongside the harbour wall.

Standing in front of one was a gathering of some twenty or thirty people, mixed ages, with some young kids, then I saw our three. They were with a tall man and a colourful women, she dressed entirely in a long flowing dress that included a balaclava type headwear, just her eyes and the top of her nose showing.

The young boys were excited about something, jumping up and down, obviously aware of the boat ride I guessed. I photographed the group, then noticed that Amil was at the edge of the group, and he was scanning it. When he noticed us he made no indication that he knew us. "That's interesting," I muttered to Jasmine, "have you seen Amil?"

"Only as you did, I guess Terry sent him to look after us."

We started to weave our way through the refugees, some squatting in groups, others just lying down on their clothes, some with their bags making a pillow for their heads. It was a sorry sight. As we neared the family, one of the boys noticed us and gave Jasmine a big grin. I also noticed that Amil was now starting to push his way through the crowds towards us. As we drew alongside the boys one pointed at Jasmine and she started to talk to their father, After some back and forth, she must have asked him if he spoke English, as he answered. "Yes I do a little."

"We are a film unit, making a documentary on the plight of refugees, your boys were with our camera men and said you expected to sail to Greece tonight. Can you tell us how you arranged it, as that will be interesting."

"I can't see camera and film people," he replied.

"Oh yes, we have left them at the other end of the harbour, your boys acted out a scene for them."

He turned towards the boys, all standing close to each other. I guess he asked them, as the tall one nodded and smiled at Jasmine.

"We met two men last night, they said we could go to Greece today when it get dusky on the middle boat there." He pointed at the three dinghies.

"Did you have to pay much?" asked Jasmine.

He replied in his own tongue. She shook her head, and asked another question, because he looked somewhat surprised, but answered, shaking his head at the same time.

They had a two way conversation for a couple of minutes, then she turned to me. "He paid a large sum last night in a room down near the harbour, all he was given was the number of the dinghy, a sort of receipt, and told to be here in the early evening when it will sail to Greece."

"Is that all?" I asked.

"Apparently, he was told they will be escorted by a professional crew, and some other refugees. They wouldn't say how many were going on that boat, but, he said, he has talked to others here who are waiting for their boat, and who will be on one of the other two."

"So it's pretty shady?"

"I think we knew it would be, but he was told not to try to come back to meet anyone at the same place. The traffickers said this, because of the Turkish police, they have to keep moving to new places each day, and they have daily trips to Greece from here."

"So we're at the right place. I wonder how Terry and Hussain are doing?"

"Let's see if we can get a bit further with him regarding the traffickers. I suggest you photograph him and his family. I will make notes of the shots, get his name, and more background, where they came from in Syria, and just how much he paid for the family to travel over. In fact, looking at the dinghies, they look to be flat bottomed, so I wouldn't think they would overcrowd any of them, especially if the weather was bad, and with any of their crew likely to be on them."

"Presumably some of theirs will be on it, to ensure it gets back here."

"Good point. I will get them to pose now as a close knit family, you do the picky job OK?"

With that she started chatting to him again and smiling, she got the boys squatting in front of their parents, I took five shots from slightly different angles, making sure that I was also including a background of others spread behind them.

Amil arrived beside us, and he started talking to the man, who apparently agreed to go with us to where he had paid his money yesterday.

We left his wife and three children and started walking alongside the harbour, until we were facing a row of houses, all in need of repair. The man led us to one in the centre of them, a sort of shop. It had some wet suits and goggles, hanging from the wall outside, and inside, there was a large woman behind a counter, which had a variety of swimming gear on it. Amil asked her something, she pointed to the door, presumably giving directions. Amil nodded his thanks and we all trooped out.

Jasmine said she seemed to be somewhat startled to be asked where the people were that organised trips for the refugees, because she quickly handed over the responsibility, and told us where we would most likely find our men.

We walked further along the side of the harbour passing Dan and Patrick, standing beside their mounted camera, gazing at the passing people, ignoring those sitting around the harbour wall. Neither of them looked as if they were enjoying the experience. Jasmine stopped with them for a minute, then she came back to us again said. "They've not seen Terry or Hussain at all."

We eventually arrived at a ramshackle building that had a door hanging by its hinges, and sloping inwards. Amil and our guide led the way into the building.

Just inside a hallway opened out into a large room, with desks positioned alongside one wall. Sitting at one of the desks were two dark skinned men. The other desks were not manned. Amil asked our Syrian if they were the people he had dealt with, and he shook his head. He then questioned the two men and one shrugged, and looked enquiringly at his friend, asking him something. They both got up from the table and looked hard at Jasmine. She talked to them and after a few seconds, one of them left the room and returned after a couple of minutes with a young blond man, whilst we all waited silently the blonde man asked Jasmine in French what she wanted. She replied in French that, we were making a documentary on the refugee situation, that much I understood. She then asked him if he spoke English, which he confirmed.

He was here in Turkey employed by the French Government. He was to report anything that was connected to the refugees getting to Europe. He was also involved whenever possible, with the people arranging the trips. Jasmine pointed out the Syrian man we had brought with us, who yesterday had paid a large sum to get himself and his family to Greece.

She then asked him if he was involved financially?

No, he wasn't, he was an observer.

"What freedom do you have with the traffickers, do you know them? Do you keep the Turkish police informed as to who they are, and the arrangement of boats to transport them?"

"I tell the police and the security services virtually all that I learn."

"But do they trust you to be involved with the organisation of the crossings?"

"I'm not involved." He stopped talking and looked at the two men. He uttered something because they both shook their heads, and pointed at us. Jasmine answered whatever their question had been.

He then said, "They are loath to be seen to be involved with the transportation."

"But they are," said Jasmine.

"Yes they are, but it's too dangerous to be seen taking money from the refugees."

"So how are the transactions done, the man we talked to a little while ago said he had met people in the ramshackle house we were visiting, and given instructions as to which dinghy he should report to."

"It's all a mix, these men are at the front of the operations, they get paid for arranging trips, they organise the crew, they always want the dinghies to come back, even though they are not expensive."

"So where does the real money come from?"

"There are people we believe in France, that finance some of the operations, that's the real reason I am here, trying to find out who, or which finance company, group or individual, is involved."

"Ok, and have you made any real progress?"

"I have some clues, and it's not too safe for me to encourage you, or other interested parties in digging, I didn't realise you have a vested interest, in addition to making a documentary."

"We see lots of refugees arriving in Greece and Italy, but never see any starting the journey. That's the most interesting part, and I guess, you must have had other groups trying to do the same as us. We are determined to see the next lot starting their journey, is it safe to do that, do you think?"

"By safe I take it you mean, will there be any attack on you, and your group here now. I will fill you in a bit more. We have a high ranking official in France that is really concerned about the whole situation here, mainly because he has a younger brother that is known to be fleecing the refugees. It is important for him to get his brother away from this situation, because, it will be detrimental to him and his position in France, if his tie to his brother is exposed. He is a prominent figure in politics. My position here is entirely due to him, and our government."

"Thank you for that, we had heard that France was interested in the situation here, and you have confirmed that. However we, with the help of our Syrian family, are now hoping to film the dinghy that they are on, and if we can, will get interviews tonight."

"Have care, make sure you are not too exposed. I know that if the Turkish Police are seen to be with you, you will not get any film, or interviews with the traffickers. What time is your family meant to be sailing?"

"We're just checking that out."

It suddenly occurred to me, following what the French guy had said, I couldn't see any reason why I should be here. Obviously the subterfuge that Maria's husband had shown, was due to his brother being involved here. I can't help Terry and his group any more, and I'm sure they see that too. I nodded to Jasmine to get a little way away from everyone.

"Jasmine, listening to the French chap has made me aware that I can't really contribute much to this now, and I'm not relevant. Obviously the French politician doesn't want any damaging publicity regarding his brothers role in trafficking, so he is going to play his cards close to the chest, and it ties in with him coming to Turkey, even though the publicity says he was going to Calais. I reckon I should leave, and let you and Terry do what you can."

"Alan, I was thinking the same thing, it was a long shot involving you anyway, so I personally don't have any objection to you leaving, but, I would like you to be on hand for photographs when the family gets loaded on to their dinghy, then I can get Amil to take you to the airport tomorrow, is that ok? In fact we may all come, as it's somehow lost its importance to us, and our government will see that we have done our bit. Maybe Terry may have something to say, but, let's discuss that tonight after the sailing."

"I guess so, but how do I explain my involvement with your cause, and the initial so called training I had with Patrick. Is it likely that your department will want to use me anymore?"

"Alan we need to talk that out with Terry, let's see if the Frenchman will want to be with us when we get the departure arranged."

We then went back towards the harbour with our man, he was obviously anxious to see that his wife and family were alright, and relieved that they were still in the same spot, where we left them.

There was quite a large crowd of refugees around them, Jasmine suggested I take some photos of the crowds which might be useful. I got out my camera, was about to start when there were shouts, certainly of anger, and one hysterical screaming. I hastily swung my camera round to see if there was a reason for it. There were three bearded dark skinned men pushing at some of the crowd that were gathered behind me. One lady was screaming and pointing at the tallest of the three, several of the crowd were staring at her, while some of the other men were facing up to the three.

One of them suddenly pulled out a long knife and started waving it round his body, this made everyone fall back from him. He was shouting at all of us, Jasmine said to me. "He's unbalanced, he's threatening to kill any non-believers, the other two are not saying anything, just basically keeping an eye on him. We need to get away from this but, let's do it slowly, best way is to back over towards the side of the crowd. We were just starting to sidle away when the knife wielder pushed his way through the crowd, and coming up close shouted something at me. I just looked blankly at him and retreated a step or two. but Jasmine says, "he wants to be photographed slicing off someone's head."

"You've got to be kidding," I ground out.

"No, I think he could be serious. I will try to talk him out of it, and suggests he stands at the front of the crowd swinging his knife, that way he will look much more important, and be seen to terrify all of us. That should also take up a bit of time, I'm sure that some of the people here will have alerted the police, or security people to what is happening. You play along and take time fixing the camera angle."

"Well I'll try, but is he listening to you. He's still swinging that damn thing around, and it's too close for comfort."

"I think he is, he's quietened down a bit, but let's see what he does when he realises I speak his language." She then walked right up to him, raised her left arm across her chest, and talked to him, pointing to a place a little ahead of the crowd.

Jasmine turned towards me as he shouted something to her, then he began slowly to move away from the crowd. Suddenly there was a frightening bang close at hand, and he fell, clutching the top of his leg. I quickly photographed him as he lay pressing his leg and shouting. Blood was already beginning to darken the skirt-like trousers he was wearing. There were more shouts, and police were grabbing the other two men. Two police pushed through to the knifeman, and the taller of the two kicked the man in his right arm, the knife to fall out of his hand.

They grabbed him, and one of them started hitting the man with his baton, as they got him to his feet and started to march him away. I was taking photos of the whole episode, he carried on shouting at the police and struggling with them.

Jasmine said. "Phew that was nasty, I wonder how he has avoided being banged up in jail anyway, if he has been threatening like that."

"Don't know but I have some shots of the whole affair."

"Didn't the police notice you doing that?"

"Don't think they too were concerned about photos at the time."

"Well you're lucky you've still got the camera, I 'm sure they wouldn't like that treatment to be publicised."

"What shall we do now?"

"Let's team up with Dan and Patrick, they may have the other family with them by now."

As we walked away from the crowd, we saw our family also walking towards the harbour where the dinghies were moored. They were talking animatedly among themselves. We had only gone a little way when we met our two, coming towards us.

"What was all the fuss about?" queried Dan.

"Oh we had a nutter wanting to chop off a head or two, and be photographed doing it. But the Police arrived just in time, and he's now with them, getting a roughing up I should imagine. I think he was a bit disturbed."

"We heard the noise and a shot, and saw a few people rushing in your direction, so thought we might catch up with some fun."

"Not too much fun Dan, have you seen Terry and the family?"

"No, we've just been hanging around."

"I guess we'd better go back to where you were, as that's where we last saw them. Also our man has taken us to where he paid for his trip. We met a Frenchman that's involved with it all. But, it must soon be time for the first group to set off, so let's keep up with our lot."

We were then stopped by a Turkish man, who talked to Jasmine at some length. She was answering his comments. He then shook her hand and wandered back towards the group where we had been.

"What was that about?" I asked.

"Apparently he was congratulating me on getting the knife wielder to move clear of the crowd, and away from us, which enabled one of his security guards to get in the shot."

"Clever old you," I smiled.

"That's me," she said.

We carried on along the harbour, our family had just stopped and were gazing at the sea, which appeared pretty calm. We got up level with the dinghies, there was quite a crowd standing along the harbour wall, I imagined they were waiting for their crew.

Suddenly there was activity, people were beginning to climb into the first dingy, Our family looked to be positioned in the middle, waiting for that one to get loaded. I couldn't see anyone ushering them in, yet obviously it had started. More and more of them we being loaded, and the dinghy was sinking with the weight. It looked to be just above the water level and with no warning it set off. I trained my camera, and took some shots, It was still light, but there appeared to be two men at the front with yellow jackets on. The crew I guessed. It was then we saw Terry with Hussain and his family plus Amil; they were queueing in front of the middle dingy.

We pushed our way to them, Hussain was deep in conversation with two men, again in faded yellow jackets. He was asking them to be filmed with their family Jasmine said, but they were refusing. They said they were told never to be filmed, and would not give any details of the routes their dinghies would take. In addition they said, they no idea if a Frenchman was involved with the financing of the dinghies.

Amil was helping Hussain with his discussion, he appeared to be getting quite heated in his approach, until eventually one of the two men waved and called across to someone else, I was taking photos as a hulking great shaven headed figure pushed his way towards them.

"This is getting dangerous," Jasmine said. "He is obviously hired help strong arm stuff. I think we should ease our way out of this. Keep taking photos Alan if you can do it, of Hussain and the two men, but watch out for muscles."

Dan had also got his handheld camera and was trying some filming. Patrick gently eased himself alongside Amil, Terry, and Hussain. I set my camera and tried two close up shots of Hussain and the two men. As I did so, I was suddenly grabbed from behind and two great muscular brown arms were wrapped around me. I struggled a bit and as I did Patrick stepped towards us and drove his elbow into the man's face, then immediately chopped him with a vicious hook to his throat. The man released me, fell down on his hands and knees and started choking and gagging.

Terry said "OK everyone let's leave this, you've got your

camera Alan, and Dan, did you get anything? We are going to upset Hussain and his family. I think it better if we leave them to it He's paid for their passage, so they should be ok, lets get at the back of the crowd and film the dinghies leaving if we can, providing we don't get any aggro from this praying gent here on his knees. Well done Patrick, but I think they may call up extra reserves, and we could end up in a battle."

I felt quite shaken from the sudden activity, but was glad that Patrick released me, obviously the brute would have grabbed the camera, and no doubt thrown it, and maybe me into the sea. We pushed our way towards the back of the throng. It occurred to me that Patrick was obviously not just a sniper. He had driven his elbow into the brutes head and the speed with which he then swung his other flat hand to hit his adam's apple was very impressive.

I guess that Terry had given up on the idea of filming any transactions, it was obvious now, that was very unlikely. From my point of view, I had taken some photos on the edge of activity and wondered what my next step would be.

We managed to get through the close-knit crowd, Dan got himself raised on a disused trolley and was aiming his movie camera on the middle dinghy. It was crowded with refugees, and very low in the water. It set off, luckily the sea was calm, had it been rough, it would have washed over the sides.

Dan continued filming until it disappeared from view. Terry had been watching Dan and the dinghy, he then said, "Let's get to the hotel and prepare for an early departure in the morning. Jasmine can you organise a flight for us, about mid-morning."

We trooped back to the hotel, hardly saying a word to each other. I suppose the drama had gone out of the situation, and we were all resigned to the fact that it had basically been a complete waste of time in our attempt to get anything really telling, in our few days here.

Dinner was a fairly sombre affair, not much was said by anyone. Terry spent some time on his phone just before we sat down, and seemed totally involved with his dinner. Jasmine said she had arranged a flight at midday, we could leave the hotel about 9.15 in the morning, so could we all be packed and ready to go at nine o'clock.

As we finished our dinner, Terry said he had had a meeting initially with Hussain and his opposite number in Turkey. After he had told the Turk who Hussain was, he and Terry apparently got together and he brought Terry up to date with the situation here. Hussain had gone off to find his family. Terry said, "all is not well here, apparently the government has instructed the police and border patrols to start using force, ie...shooting if necessary, on the border with Syria. They want to stop all refugees coming in. They are also closely inspecting lorries and cars, making it almost impossible for anyone trying to get away from Syria. Also apparently, the government's decisions have created some difference of opinion with the armed forces, and there is a coup likely to take place very soon. So his advice to us is, to get out, because if the coup does take place, most of the airports will be closed down and life here can change dramatically. He also said that Russia has now started to help Assad, and are at present bombing Aleppo where many of the rebels are in command, plus some Isis are near at hand. So it's all in the melting pot at present, and I'm pleased we are leaving."

We all absorbed Terry's information, I certainly looked forward to getting out, and back to my normal way of life. Did I want to be exposed like this, what if they offer me more work?

I had a couple of beers with Dan and Patrick, discussed

Patricks treatment of the strong arm man, and he simply said. "He was keen on you Alan, had you in his arms, I thought a good chop might stop his amorous approach."

I smiled. "Thanks Patrick. I would have done the same, but he had me wrapped in his arms, no doubt it was my beauty that drove him wild with desire."

We chatted a while about the whole episode, and travelling with refugees. "A good title for a book" I suggested.

Dan said, "Why not write it Alan, you have a taste for drama."

We all went to bed quite early. I tried to get a signal on my mobile but it was dead, so I read a bit and wondered what my next job would be. To think, I had only been in Turkey a few days. The many hours driving, mainly looking at refugees meant, I had hardly taken any exercise at all; that worried me and I resolved to make up for that as soon as we got back to London. I also wondered if they would want me for any other work now that the Maria contact was not of any real interest to them.

The next morning, we set off early and were soon at the airport. We all said goodbye to Amil and were quickly moved through the loose security and loaded into our private jet. At least that aspect of my trip was impressive. Three hours later we landed at Biggin Hill, and were cleared in minutes.

On the way back, Terry gave a sort of de-briefing, suggesting that we keep all that we had seen and heard to ourselves, and certainly, no discussion with any newspapers. He would see what Dan had produced and he also wanted hard copies of all that I had taken.

CHAPTER 20

Getting back to town they dropped me at my studio. I felt myself settling into a kind of daydream about my experience. Terry thanked me, also saying he would like a meeting in the next couple of days, to discuss all aspects of our journey. Patrick and Dan said lets meet up, and Jasmine said she would call tomorrow, to fix up a meeting. I thanked them all for the experience and told them, I would try to get in touch with my French lady, tell her what I had been doing without giving any indication of the government involvement. Terry asked me not to contact her until after I had seen him. As they drove off, I wondered if my initial meeting with Maria, and the fact her husband seemed to be somewhat shady, had caused the whole episode to be created. and, if the expenses for the trip would be ignored.

Then I suddenly realised, I had left my car at the safe house, I must check with Terry or Jasmine as to how I should get it back.

In my studio, I found a neat pile of letters on my desk, and a short note from Rachel.

Alan I don't think your mobile is working, I have left messages for you, and expected replies, but silence.

When you get back call me at home when you read this.. XX

Oh, maybe a problem. I put my equipment in its normal place, and then telephoned her. "Hi, I'm back in one piece and ready to give my all. Anything exciting happened?"

"Alan, I hope you're feeling strong. I've been visited twice by two men asking about you, what you are doing, and they wouldn't confirm why they needed to know. I said you were out of the office on a job, and not sure where or when you would be back, was that the right thing to do?"

"Yes, were they French do you know, or Brits?"

"Don't know, They were there last Wednesday, and again on Friday, and they frightened me."

"It's Ok Rachel, no need to be frightened, I'm back and I will check out the two possible parties that could have had an interest in what I was doing. Can you come in tomorrow and we can have a comforting lunch." I settled into my office and started reading through the mail, but couldn't really concentrate on the various letters, as my mind was still very much caught up in thinking about Turkey, and the refugees. I wondered if Hussain and his family made Greece or Italy, or where ever they were headed. It was also interesting that he said that he wanted to get to Germany. He hardly mentioned England or anywhere else as I recalled. I must watch tele and see if there is any news on boats arriving to the Greek islands. One of my letters was from Maria. I started reading it with a certain anticipation, Was it going to be honest?

Dear Alan, I trust by now you have settled back in London, and maybe forgotten about me, I just wanted you to know that I did enjoy our meeting, and our time together in Nice. I'm sure you felt the same, it was written on your face, and I'm sorry we never had time to get even closer in Paris. You must think I am completely controlled by my husband, because I was very much on edge when we met in your hotel. I wondered if I had been followed, but apparently not, so let me know how you are, and what plans you might have for us to meet. Until then I seal this letter with a kiss I remember as a schoolgirl we used to say. Swalk. Wish I was young again. xxx

Maria

Now that is interesting, she may know I've been to Turkey, I'm sure the blond Frenchman will have told her husband that we were there. I wondered when she had written the letter, there was no date on it. I won't contact her until I've seen Terry, even though the inner me would like to. There were several other letters, a couple of cheques, and some sales literature on a variety of products. Nothing of any real interest until I found one from my Aussie ex-girlfriend.

Hi Alan, Job's been put off for a couple of months, will let you know the revised dates as soon as I have them, till then keep your pecker up... You naughty boy. Love 'Constance Cummings'... Thought that would keep your mind recalling our last night together.

XXX

I tried to contact Kevin. But his PA said he was shooting a commercial, I left my number with her and got a call back promise. I decided I would go to my flat in Southwark for the rest of the day. I felt pretty rung out. I guess the inactivity, and constant travel had made me somewhat tired. But inwardly I am excited, not sure why, but, I think, something pretty big is on the horizon for me. I get home, throw all my things on the settee, and decide. it's a run round one of the parks. Not been to Battersea for a while, that will do. After nearly an hours run, when I got back, hot and trembling a bit, I found my telephone light was flashing, a message. I pressed the play.

Hello Alan, I got your number from your French friend, and just wanted to meet up for a chat, and have a message for you... I hardly heard the rest of his message. other than his name, Peter, and telephone number, as he finished.

What is this? Could it be a set up? maybe her husband's got someone to straighten me out. I resolved that I wouldn't call him. I had a shower, then sat on my sofa, trying to work out why this was happening. I had her letter, no mention of anyone calling me. I wouldn't take the bait, if he really wanted to meet, he would call again. I also thought I might ask Patrick, where and how he got his real training. Cos if I am to be exposed through any new work, I would like to be able to really defend myself. I had done a bit of boxing when I was at school, but that was kid's stuff. Patrick showed me what the real world was about.

The idea of a good meal was attractive, also as I had been sharing my time with the group, a bit of isolation appealed. I'd had nothing to eat other than the mezes on the airplane all day. I went to my favourite Indian restaurant off the Kings road, and succeeded in filling myself, with loads of Indian beer. On getting home I opened up my computer to catch up on my missing days. Some twenty odd messages floated up. The usual offers of cheap holidays. Eating at Carlucios, a five star Hotel in the lake district, and a sex invitation, well that's a new one. I also had a long letter from the wife of a dear friend, who had recently died in USA. She was tempted to come to London in a couple of months, would I be able to house her for a few nights.. She said she had lots of loose ends to tie up with the remnants of his business...I also had two messages from my agent, one about the commercial in

Nice. The French company had been very satisfied with my work, and would certainly use me when applicable on any future jobs. They were also going to expand my bank account via BACs, and wanted my banking swift number. Well my agent had that, perhaps he has informed them. He had also heard of the Aberdeen job, and wanted to know the details. Maybe Rachel had told him. But, I had got that direct, don't think he should get any credit for that. So nothing to take up too much time, or anything to get worried about. I wrote to the friend in the USA.

The next morning when Rachel arrived, we talked about the two men that had visited her. I told her I had a message from someone claiming to be a friend of someone I had met in France, so there are a few links to be sorted. The visits from the men concerned me. I wondered what they were leading to. She couldn't throw any light on their visit. It was while I was talking to her that Terry telephoned. He wanted to see me for a quick lunch today, and gave me the name of the restaurant where we could meet. I had promised Rachel lunch today, and said I would take her out as soon as I could, but it was obviously important for Terry to call me so soon.

When I arrived he was sitting at the back of the room, watching the door. I sidled over and he immediately got down to business. "Have you brought your pictures that you took, or have you brought the camera so we can see them?" I assured him that they were on camera, I'd not had time to get anything printed, but what's the hurry, why the sudden meeting.

"You did say as we parted, that you would call in the next couple of days, has something developed from our visit?"

"Patrick said, you had shown an interest in working with us, and would also like some training in self-defence, and, presumably attack, why would you want to do that?"

"I was impressed by Patricks speed of movement, and his obvious ability to keep trouble at bay. Perhaps if I do get to work with you, unarmed combat, I think they used to call it that, could be a part of your activities, and would be very useful to defend oneself." I was getting a bit James Bond there, but Terry didn't bat an eyelid, and said.

"OK I'm sure we can find work for you but, I would like to see what you have produced from Turkey before we go any further."

"Before I show you the photos, why the sudden meet?"

"Patrick has asked if you would like to accompany him on a trip he has to make to Kenya. It could be a bit dangerous, he would be an investigating journalist, and you would be his photographer."

"Why a bit dangerous, what does it entail?"

"There are three or four governments that are looking at some combined activity there. We believe some groups are quite strong but, we, and the others, are getting an operational special services unit to free three of our nationals that have been grabbed. They are threatening to sell them to Isis unless a great deal of money is provided for their release."

"Oh and how can Patrick discover where they are, and why they were grabbed?"

"That's the big question, where they are being held? Are you up to being exposed to a bit of danger?"

"Let me think about that, also presumably I shall be paid for my other journey with you to Turkey?"

"Yes, Jasmine will be in touch tomorrow with some good news for you."

"Terry before I met you as you know, I was somehow involved with a French lady, and there are questions I would like answered. On my second day in Nice with the lady, I was somewhat threatened on the phone in my room. When I went to meet with this person, I saw him being led off by the police. Have you any idea what that was about?"

"Yes we checked it out when we took you on board. The chap was a small time crook, and he had noticed you and your lady and, recognising her, thought he might have a story to sell. The frogs police got to him in time, and banged him up, He's now out on the streets, no doubt trying to find other juicy morsels he can inflame."

"So that's all settled is it? Then tell me, on my telephone at home, one of my messages was telling me to keep away from my French lady, what's that about?"

"Don't know, but we will try to find out. Right now, because of the update on possible terror attacks we are conscripting people for our work. This is really asking you if you are willing, and prepared to join up. You would still get time for some of your own work, but, the only stipulation is, that if we come urgently calling, you must be ready to go to wherever we need you."

"Do I have to give you an answer now?"

"No. Let Jasmine know tomorrow, and we will go from there. Let's look at the photos."

CHAPTER 21

Terry enthused over some of my work, and after a half hour, he said he would like to study them with Jasmine, and could he keep the camera overnight? She can return it tomorrow when you meet. I was initially reluctant to do that, as I had some other work on it, some of which I wasn't sure I wanted him to see. But…

"Yes OK, get her to call me at the studio this afternoon. Before we leave can you get my car delivered back to me I left it at the house in Kent."

"Sure but I will need the key."

I gave it to him and we left each other, I wandered back to my studio, as I walked, I wondered where this might lead. Was I ready to get involved, did I want to go to Kenya, I went there once and was horrified with the roads that I had to either drive on, or had the courage to be driven. I remember one episode, having gone to photograph Flamingo's at one of the large lakes, we were driving back towards the capital, Nairobi, and our driver, being a chatty chap, was holding forth on the state of the roads. Saying how dangerous they were, with the sudden drop off the tarmac on either side, when we were overtaken by a speeding black Peugeot. Our man said, "He's pushing it." Some few miles further on, we had to slow down, as there was an obvious accident, the Peugeot was lying on its side, and there were several medics I guess, dragging people out of the car. Our driver didn't stop. He took an angle and drove off the road, giving the accident a wide berth, then bounced back regaining the road, and we sped on our way. On querying him as to why he did that, he said, "never stop at an accident, if you do, the police, or medics will insist on putting any injured people in your car, and you have to take them to the nearest hospital. Accidents are bad news for everyone here, and we get plenty of them."

So I will see what Jasmine has to say tomorrow. I was looking forward to being alone with her. That didn't happen in Turkey, she kept herself withdrawn. Was that I wondered, her usual way of life. Or, was she so wrapped up in our journeying, and, perhaps, Terry has some influence on her attitudes when working with new people. But, she seemed to be the same with Patrick and Dan. She was certainly attractive and had a body to appreciate. Hey wait a minute. I had better get control of my mind. But, I was feeling a bit fruity, it's been a while since I've had the comfort of my Aussie model. I had a quick coffee on my way back, and then tried to catch up on my post. It was whilst I was reading a heart-warming account of my sister rescuing a dog from a rabbit hole, that the telephone rang, and it was Jasmine. "Hi Alan, can we meet for a quick lunch tomorrow? I know you use the Ebury Wine Bar, can we meet there, say about twelve forty five? I will bring your camera with me. Terry and I are going to peruse some of your Turkish work today, but, I'm looking forward to seeing you out of travelling gear."

"Thanks, I will wear my very best blue trousers, and blue shoes, then, maybe, I can sing some blues for you."

"I can't wait for that, see you tomorrow, Oh, will you book a table?"

"Sure." Well, that settles it, she is human after all. I smiled to myself. She was never flippant on our few days of travel, this could be fun, except, I was probably going to be interviewed by her, albeit over a 'quick lunch,' she had said.

We met the next day, she was there sitting at a table when I arrived, looking very attractive, wearing a yellow jacket and purple sweater. She got up and we kissed, well we 'air kissed,' sat down, and she immediately said. "Some good work in your photos Alan. Terry and I both thought you had interpreted much of the disillusion and hopelessness of the refugees, and you had captured one or two traffickers, plus that incident with the knife wielder, so they could be very useful."

"I tried to vary my pictures, but it was difficult because of the pressure on time, and only a few were willing to pose. In addition, there were few opportunities to get close enough to any traffickers, to get a real image, however, if you think we can use any, that's fine."

"Good," she said. A waiter came up and we ordered gin and tonics, that amused me, then ordered lunch, very simple for us both. I said "I have some questions though, and Terry did say you could confirm anything."

"Fine go ahead."

"I'm interested in payment for the past couple of weeks, And, if you think I can fit in with some regular work, we need to get an understanding of what form of contract will I have, and timing, when will I be needed etc?"

"Alan as you know, we are really trying right now to attract more people to the service, and they may be very different in their talents. At present we, the country, is very exposed to terrorist activities. We would be very happy for you to be involved and, Patrick has said you were interested, and would also like to get more physical training, his sort of work."

"Yes I've given it a good deal of thought, and, maybe, I'm might be willing to get more involved." Our lunch arrived and for a few minutes we were quiet.

"I have a cheque for you Alan, and I have a date for you to go to the safe house, where you went previously. As you know Patrick has asked for you to go to Kenya with him, that's quite pressing at the moment, so can I suggest, if you really want to be involved, an intensive week training, and then off with him."

"I need a bit of time to clear up some outstanding work through my studio, and I need to get my PA to also clear some time, so the place is occupied and active."

"Of course, do you know anything of Kenya?"

"Yes, I had a job there some time ago, wasn't too impressed, but met an interesting chap when flying out, who claimed to be the worlds most travelled man, and he loved Kenya. At the time was trying to rescue the white hippo. He also said that Kenya was so fertile, that if you stuck your thumb in the ground, it would grow. I do enjoy a good tale, and he had a bucketful."

"You obviously know it's changed a great deal, and is not as safe generally, as it was some twenty years ago."

"Hasn't just about everywhere changed?, and not for the better."

"Sure, but since the terrorist threat has grown, it's as much exposed to danger, as other African countries."

"Jasmine, do you have many interests other than work? I never really got a chance to talk to you on the Turkish trip, but wondered if you spend all your time as a slave to the job, if I can call it that."

"Alan, is this a chat up line?"

"Maybe, but I am genuinely interested in getting to know a bit more about you."

"Why"

"Now, you've caught me on the hop, as we say in Norfolk."

"Alan I live alone, some time ago I gave myself hook line and sinker to a stinker. He took me for a ride, since then I've very much kept to myself. I have a lovely flat, I get it cleaned regularly, I have a full fridge, a comfortable bed, and believe it or not, I am very happy. And I do have other interests as you are querying, which I believe, I mentioned to you. I play snooker, and am pretty good at it. I also play backgammon, I've been known to play a mean hand of poker, as many in our line of business does, and I love the theatre, Now how does that sit with you for an answer?"

"Wow, I'm impressed."

"Why are you impressed?"

"You certainly cover that side of your life well. You are also very professional In your work ethics. You were highly organised in Turkey. What's your relationship with Terry?"

"We work together, we have had a few jobs over the years, and we understand what we want from each other, and the job. He's also a dedicated workaholic, in case you didn't notice."

"Jasmine I will be completely straight with you, I have a pretty good life in London, I'm earning well, I also have a very comfortable flat in Southwark, and my work satisfies me in general, but, I'm thirty now, and deep down, I would like a bit more excitement. For the last couple of weeks I have been it seems, flat out in this dodgy way of life. I don't mean that as something dishonest, but the intrigue of the French bit, the travel in Turkey, seeing another side of life with the refugee situation, that has fired me to do something out of the rut. I'm sure I can add more, but initially I would like to get some toughening up physically, and then become more involved. I don't particularly want to give up my

189

studio, or some of the regular work that I'm contracted for, but its spasmodic, and, I would have time to devote to your organisation, with the proviso that I can still be independent. Does that make sense?"

"Need to think about that Alan. In the main, when we conscript, we look for dedication to the cause, official secrets etc., You know that you were brought in because of your French contact, well that proved pointless, although we are still interested in your ladies involvement, as that seemed a bit shady. How much time would you need for your own business, say monthly?"

"Difficult to be precise, but, it varies. Usually, I and my PA scout for business, then there is the recommendation aspect. Some months I can be very busy, others, generally following up work I have done. Basically how much call does your organisation have for photographic work, cos that is the determining thing, I guess that's all I can really offer."

"You'd be surprised, Like Patrick, when he was in his sniper role, he could be static for hours, maybe days. Perhaps the same could be said of photographic work, waiting for the opportunity, could be the same thing, long periods of watching and waiting. Now that might put you off."

"So no dead letter drops and secret holes in walls. Maybe I should forget the whole thing Jasmine, lets meet occasionally for a game of snooker at my club, and you can let me win. I play the game."

"Where do you play?"

"I bet you're a member of the 'Spy's club' in Pall Mall. I am a member of one there too, a little bit along from yours."

"And you have a lady professional."

"How do you know that?"

"Because we sometimes get invitations."

"Well, well. Yes, and she's pretty good."

"Have you played with her?"

"Couple of times, she gave me six blacks start, and beat me by 40 odd."

"Alan, enough of this chatter, lets sum up where we are."

"I think I've told you my side, what can you offer?" She felt in her handbag. "Here is your cheque." She handed me an envelope. I casually opened it and was quite surprised by the amount. So they can pay well, I thought.

"Thanks Jasmine. Glad to see you are still using cheques, they are going out of fashion they tell me."

"Not with us yet, but they will soon I'm assured. OK we would like you to work with us, initially on an, as required basis."

"Fine, OK, I need a couple of days to get all my things arranged, then I can have say a week in training, and then Kenya, is that acceptable?"

"I will email you a contract spelling out full details for you within the job, you email it back, confirming your acceptance, copy it, and sign where required, I will arrange that you start at the safe house next week."

We both looked at our empty lunch plates, I signalled the waiter, then tipped back my water and got up to go. "I look forward to a game with you," I said. She nodded, smiled and held out her hand.

"Welcome Alan." And with that walked quickly to the door, I ambled after her and watched her stride off into the very slight rain that was beginning to make an impression. I stood contemplating our conversation, I wondered, was I being irrational, was I jumping into the pool without wearing my armbands? I then surprised myself by calling loudly, "Jasmine, wait."

She turned round and stood, eyeing me with a grin on her face. As I panted up to her she said, "I knew you were going to do that."

"Well you knew better than me, I surprised myself by

suddenly realising I wanted to say, 'dinner tomorrow night', keep me sane, for my training the day after. Is that a yes I see hovering around your eyes? and, do you have ESP?"

"Yes"

"Where do you live, I'm in Southwark, very close to the Globe theatre, I have a balcony looking out over the Thames."

"Oh trying to influence me are you. I also look out over the Thames, close to Tower Bridge, I have a large mortgage. That looks out over the Thames. Keeps me sane."

"What about Le Pont de la Tour?"

"That's full of impressionable MP's and slick city boys, too expensive, when you have a large mortgage. Do you know the Blue Print, that looks over the Thames, as it seems to be our theme, and it's raining. The Blue Print is literally three minutes walk from my flat, can we meet there?"

"Sure seven thirty, and I shall come in my best blue trousers. I'll book a table looking at the Thames!!"

"I look forward to that, share the cost?"

"No, you have a large mortgage. I have invited you." She swung round with a smile on her face, I watched her stride off, never a backward glance. Am I a hopeless romantic, why would she look back. I turned and found I too was smiling. When I got back to the studio Rachel was there on the phone as I walked in. She was nodding and waved me to sit down in front of her. She thanked the caller, and then turned her attention to me. "Alan, just had a call from a Maurice Bent, sometimes known as Peter. He said you had been to his offices recently, and he would like a chat. He said he had called you a couple of times, as he had your home number from your French friend. I told him you were out, but would let you know when you returned. "Thanks Rachel." She gave me his number. I wonder why he's followed up my visit, I thought, someone having the home number was a bit mysterious, presumably Maria had given it to him. I called the number, a woman answered. Yes, she would get Maurice, what was my name? Having given it to her, I waited, and a few seconds later he came on. "Alan, can I call you that? You kindly left a parcel here from your friend in Paris, she has been in touch and is coming to London next week, and had hoped she could meet you."

"Why would she ask you to let me know this?, she has my home telephone number, which she has obviously given to you."

"I know, She probably thought it better to use me as an intermediary, knowing who she is, than risking any repercussions from calling you direct."

"I don't understand that. You could tell her that I would be very pleased to see her, but unfortunately I am away from London next week, and can't change the contract I have."

"OK. I will tell her that, thanks."

"One thing bothers me, On my answer machine you said your name was Peter, what was that about?"

"When I started up our company, being in the travel business, everything has to be correct, because of the guarantees etc., and I gave my name, Maurice Bent. But several people I met, found the name funny, and would laugh when I told them, so my middle name is Peter, I tend to use that for all friends, that's all."

"Hmm. Maybe Maurice Bent is funny. I will think about that.. Thanks anyway." I hung up and thought about the name. Ah well it takes all sorts. I thought about not seeing her. I hadn't as yet fully thought out if I really wanted to get involved with our secret services. I enjoyed, or rather I had enjoyed my work. Meeting Maria and the follow up to that had somehow got me thinking. I would like to have a more exciting life. I will talk to Jasmine tomorrow night, maybe she could point me in the right direction. I suddenly found I was really looking forward to that. Did I really want to be involved with a married lady? I know the thought of a closer relationship with Maria had stimulated me, but, Jasmine could also stimulate me. She had warned me off I guess, with the description of her previous lover, but I wonder how long she has been without any real relationship? She seemed warm enough to my suggestion of dinner. I must play this slowly. With that thought I put my mind to my own work, there were several things I had to follow up.

CHAPTER 22

The following evening I had a shower, cut my toenails, well, you never know… and made myself as beautiful as I could. I was definitely excited at the prospect of entertaining Jasmine. I wonder if she will be anticipating the evening? I have the feeling that she devotes herself to work, and the social doesn't attract her, but then, I could be completely wrong. In any event, she seemed quite keen to meet for dinner and, presumably her previous experience has made her very wary of getting involved.

The Blue Print wasn't that far for me to walk, I always enjoy walking alongside the Thames, so I set off, allowing plenty of time. When I arrived, I asked the maître'd. if we could have a window table as I had requested that when booking, and we were both water babies. He looked me up and down, smiled, and said. "Do you really mean, 'Babies?"

"Well this is a first date, and I want it to be perfect, can you see to that?"

"Sir, I will do my best."

He led me to a table, overlooking the Thames. Pointed to the menu lying on the table, and left me. The background music level was quite high. This surprised me, as the last time I had been there, one could hardly hear anything because of the loud conversations going on, no doubt inspired by the loud music.

Maybe I am slipping out of the young life and way of communicating Will see if it disturbs Jasmine, then I can pull the big boy and ask for it to be lowered. I also asked for a glass of champagne, which I would toy with until she arrived. The place wasn't very full yet, but it's quite early, and I know a lot of the city boys eat here, so the noise level is usually high.

There was a very old couple just across from me, they were both studying the menu with looks at each other, and some hesitation. They had already sent the waiter away once. He was now hovering again. As I watched them, I saw Jasmine arrive. The maître'd. was all smiles, as she looked around and waved at me. She handed her scarf to a waiter and wandered over with the maître'd. I leapt to my feet. She was radiant, absolutely beautiful in a dark, turquoise dress that fitted her like a glove, and, showed a bit of cleavage. Her pink jacket finished her ensemble beautifully.

I grabbed both her hands and kissed them. "You're looking absolutely radiant, what a few days in the sun will do to real beauty, and, would you like a glass of champagne?"

"Yes please." looking at the maître'd.

"Of course," he said.

We sat. I gazed at her completely stunned by her beauty. "Jasmine, I may just sit here tongue tied and feast my eyes on you."

"Steady on Alan, I might like a little conversation, and, can I please ask, no mention of Turkey, refugees and work? Is that a nod, or is your head a bit loose?"

I struggled to concentrate, she was so different from the Jasmine I had spent a few days with. I had gazed at her a bit whilst on our travels, but, now, she had her hair slightly waved, her eyes were alive and I just wanted to hug her.

"Jasmine, your wish is my command."

The champagne arrived and we toasted each other with a 'Here's to the future.'

"Alan are you going to be subservient all night, looking like a love sick calf, or can we eat a bit, talk a bit and enjoy it."

"I thought you were going to say, and enjoy a bit. That's an old Norfolk expression for sweltering youth."

"Naughty boy, just behave yourself."

"I am trying, we never really got a chance to talk on our travels, you notice, so far I've not mentioned any of the things you said were verboten."

"That's a short sentence and even shorter time. It was work Alan, and we were very much thrown together, but, after you invited me for dinner, I really found I was looking forward to it, and, maybe with a little light relief. I have been so tied down with work of late that, I've hardly been out for a real meal for some time. So thank you."

I smiled at her. "Let's have a look at the menu. It's been quite some time since I've eaten here."

We were quiet for a few minutes as we studied the menu.

"Are you a three course man Alan, or are you watching your slender waist?"

"You've been studying me have you?" I grinned.

"Only in passing."

"I'm usually happy with two, but often after having two, the puds might impact on my mind."

We both decided on mains of fish, so I ordered a Chablis, and we settled back to talk.

The Chablis arrived with a little amuse bouche.

"Alan tell me your history, I know you come from Norfolk, but that's all I know, how did you get to London."

I told her the full story, it took me back a bit to Maria, asking the same question. When I had finished I asked for her background.

"Its pretty humdrum. Private school in Sussex. Then Cambridge, where I was invited to join the mob I work for, and being told at the beginning, don't get too close to any workmates."

"Really, that's a bit limiting isn't it ? and I guess a bit big brother, and, that's the quickest life story achievements I've ever heard."

"Gosh, that's a bit nineteen eighty four from you."

Food arrived, and we were quiet again. Our talk through dinner initially centred around the quality and presentation of the food. We had a short appreciation of politics, and were both concerned about the USA, The World, and the Middle East. We discovered we were both great lovers of Hockney. Our own Artist. She was a member of the RA. The Donmar, as I was, and she often went as a member to the National Theatre. We had both seen Saint Joan recently, at the Donmar, and we found we had much to talk about. The Chablis found a welcome route and as we talked it was soon empty. I ordered another, She seemed to agree to that. We were then asked if deserts interested us. She said she was quite content and I agreed. We had coffee and slowly finished the Chablis. I asked if she would like a limoncello and virtually as I said it, the maître'd. came up, and offered us both the same thing, which we readily accepted. The evening had, it seemed flashed past, it was nearly ten o'clock. I was feeling very comfortable with her, and hoped she felt the same way.

She suddenly asked. "Alan would you like to come to my flat, and have a late night warmer, it's only a couple of minutes away."

"You bet, I'm shivering in anticipation, and one of the things you said earlier about not getting involved with your workmates, resonated with me... but then, I'm not really working with you, and, you are a loner, or so you said. I do feel very comfortable with you though, and I'm enjoying our time together, maybe we could find some fertile ground! As we say in Norfolk. That would make me decide not to join your mob, as you call them."

"Alan it's a bit early for that sort of talk, I'm also enjoying our evening, but, don't try to rush things, let's just drift, and see if anything comes from this."

"Ok. I paid the bill, was a bit surprised by the percentage service charge they now included but, what the hell, I was feeling good, should be after all the wine we'd consumed. We walked down the stairs and out of the restaurant. I took her hand and guided her towards the rail overlooking the Thames.

"Let's gaze at the Thames; I love London's magic at night, especially on the river. Tower Bridge looks wonderful, and all the lights on the other side are bewitching."

She looked up at me, smiled and said. "Alan are you being romantic?"

We were standing close and she was inches away from me, with her face upturned, I leant forward and kissed her, she responded, Her lips were so soft and warm. I sank into their warmth.

"I'm feeling totally alive."

She smiled and said "There you go again, you old Norfolk lover."

We drew back a little and I murmured, "That was something else, phew I'm steaming!"

"We could try that again if you're up to it."

I held her close, I think I am really up for it, your lips are the most sumptuous, absorbing, smoothness, cloaked in expectation, I have ever known."

"Alan, you've been reading love stories I bet."

"It's called inspiration, and you're responsible."

"Helped with the wine?"

"Ah, now there's a point, shall we go for that late night drink you promised?"

She smiled, turned round, and gave a little tug to my hand. As we walked, swerving a little, and definitely not in a straight line, it was the drink, I tried to assure her that I was a capable, to be trusted fella, and led her, not knowing which way it was to her flat. She tugged a bit and pointed in the direction we should follow. Within a few minutes we were entering a fairly modern looking entrance hall, with glass doors and a bell push on its right side. I was really excited and looking forward to getting to her flat, I wonder how we will get back to the recent closeness was my overriding thought.

We were going up to the fourth floor I noticed, when she pressed her number in the lift, got out and just to our right, she fumbled a bit with her bag, produced a key, and we were in. The entrance hall was short, there were four doors. Two on the left, and two right, we went straight through and were then in a large sitting room, with French doors onto a patio. It looked very comfortable and large to my slightly fuddled mind. The main sofa was covered in beautiful cushions.

"This is lovely" I said, "and I can see the Thames glistening out there." She nodded, and pushed me towards a sofa.

"Take the weight off your feet Alan, and what do you want to drink?"

"Can you believe, I would love a large cup of mint tea?"

"Hello, is this you, Dr Who?" She smiled.

"Yes, I noticed on our way here that I needed to refresh my balance, and a mint tea would be right up my street."

"Do you know, I'm going to join you." She took off her jacket, I feasted my eyes on her figure, it wasn't voluptuous, or sensuous, but in her lovely dress, her hair tumbling down to her shoulders, she looked magnificent, and I told her so.

"Flatterer," and she went out to make the tea.

I sat quietly contemplating what I should do or say, when she returned. I could only think of getting close again and putting my, what seemed to me to be, oversized lips on hers.

After a few minutes she came in with two cups, put them both down on a coffee table, and hitching up her dress, came and sat on me with her legs open wide, her face was close up to me and she kissed me fully on the lips. As we progressed, her tongue darted in and out of my mouth. I was thrilled and her close proximity really aroused me, I wrapped my arms round her, pulled her close and we kissed passionately for some minutes. I wondered if she had any knickers on, but couldn't tell, as her skirt was so rumpled at the back, then she leant back and with a great grin said. "Alan you know how to kiss, that was beautiful."

I took a few seconds to regain my breath. "Yours were pretty good too, so good I've forgotten my tea."

"Oh that," she said, "it will probably douse your libido."

"Do you want that?" I asked.

"Not for a moment, I just got carried away with your beauty."

"You say the sexiest things."

"Let's go into the bedroom."

I needed no encouragement, we both picked up a cup and I followed her out of the sitting room.

We entered the first door on the left. It was quite a large bedroom with a king sized bed. "That's a lot of bed for one pretty lady."

"I like my space, let me undress you."

I gulped, took a swig of my tea, then put it down on a table and raised my arms over my head, "Is that you surrendering?"

"Absolutely."

She took her time, and I was left standing straight in all departments. She stepped back a little and looking me all over said. "Magnificent Alan. now undress me."

I unbuttoned the rest of her dress and slid it off her back, she had knickers on, so I had been dreaming.

When I had removed everything, I gently pulled her close and we locked our arms round each other, she put her feet on mine and I, lifting her with each step, walked slowly towards the bed. I hesitated. "Do I need"

"No, I'm prepared."

We made sweet love, and afterwards, lying facing each other, she said. "Alan, It's been a long time, I hope you don't think this could be a regular 'one night stand' for me."

"Not for a moment, we have spent several days together, not really talking about anything other than what was happening around us. Tonight has been so easy and relaxing, I also I think we have much in common, and I think we were both ready to get to where we are now. I can't think of anything more beautiful than what has happened," I stroked her face," and you are so beautiful, I can't get enough of you."

She put her arms round me and pressed her face against my chest. I stroked her hair and felt completely at one with her. After a few moments she said, "Alan, I'm going to be totally honest with you, I really do believe you thought you might be doing something challenging and exciting by being involved with us, You are a very good photographer, as I said earlier, you had meaningful photos, and great coverage of the refugee situation when you were able, but, I don't think you had thought it through to suggest that you could be more physical. I think Patrick impressed you with his technique of dealing with trouble, that's his role. But, your personality shouts, 'calm'. So I suggest your wanting to get involved with some of our activities that we have, would be wrong for you. Please don't misread me, but I think you should stay as you are. You're successful, talented and, if we did call on you to cover anything which we think would be suitable, perhaps that would satisfy you." She then laughed. "It also means I might get to see a bit of you without any warning off. If, of course you wanted to see me again."

"Wow, after that little lecture I am left with egg on my face. I have over the last two days, tried to put the past couple of weeks in perspective. Yes, I've enjoyed the exposure, but, I don't think I'm cut out to be a roughneck. I'm just a 'calm fella' and a coward really, can't say 'boo to a goose'. Old Norfolk expression, and somewhat aware of you. If it's perfectly possible to have feelings for someone in a short time, cos that's me!!"

"You clever old thing, you've seen through me, I'm going to give you the time of your life, so stay calm, and enjoy it."

Much later, I woke to find her curled up against me, I rolled over and saw it was seven thirty. My mouth was dry from the drink and my activity. I saw the tea cup on the table and slipped out of bed to find I had a little cold tea left. As I was drinking it she gave a slight moan, and peered out from the bed. "You're up, what's the time?", I told her, and she said, "Glad I made my first appointment at ten o'clock. Come back to bed."

I crawled in, she wriggled over to me, and ran her hands over my chest and body. We started kissing and, as we were now both fully awake. She said, "Let's have a shower together." We walked hand in hand into her spacious bathroom, there was a huge shower and she pushed me into it. She got a blue and white shower cap, and slipped it on. "What do you think of that, does it turn you on?"

"I don't need a shower cap to turn me on, step in and I will soap you everywhere." I moistened the soap and started on her back, then turned her round and soaped her breasts, I pulled her to me and rubbed against her. We slithered around for a couple of minutes, then she said, "Let me do you."

She took up the large soap and also started on my back, I was getting very excited, especially when she told me to bend forward and soaped my crevice. Then as she turned me round and soaped me everywhere. She said, "Alan you're getting lathered. I can see it." We then had a wonderful knee trembler. As yet not a drop of water had been let loose on us. She reached for, and turned on the switch and a great stream of cold water poured out of the big shower head. I shouted, and went to grab her but she stepped back and turned the handle further, warm flooded down on us. "I bet that cold water woke your dormant soul," she said, "did you enjoy the cold bit?"

"Sheer joy." I said. We stepped out and she gave me a huge green bath towel, as we dried, we were both smiling at each other. Having dried between my toes I said, "Jasmine, this has been the most wonderful night, and I am horrified that I still don't know your name."

"Alan you said at some point that you wanted more excitement in your life. Do you think the last few weeks have given you that?"

"My beauty, it has. It's been a slice of life, no, a slice of excitement."

"You could write a book calling it that," she said.

"Perhaps I will."

31993539R00116

Printed in Great Britain
by Amazon